D1715973

Sweet Death

Sweet Death

Bill Waggoner

Walker and Company
New York

First published in the United States of America in 1992
by Walker Publishing Company, Inc.
Published simultaneously in Canada by Thomas Allen & Son
Canada, Limited, Markham, Ontario

Library of Congress Cataloging-in-Publication Data
Waggoner, Bill.
Sweet Death / Bill Waggoner.
p.   cm.
ISBN 0-8027-3208-9
I. Title.
PS3573.A355S94   1992
813'.54—dc20   91-25329
CIP

Printed in the United States of America
2 4 6 8 10 9 7 5 3 1

THIS BOOK IS DEDICATED TO THE
MEMORY OF JOE PHILLIPS, BEN
DAW, AND CHARLES BENNETT.
ALL COLLEAGUES WHO WERE
TAKEN FROM US TOO SOON.

Sweet Death

1

Personal Demons

THE OLD MAN IS lying facedown in a slowly expanding pool of his own blood. The left half of his face is now a part of the new low-tar cigarette display. Not six feet away lies the remains of his ten-year-old grandson. A 12-gauge at point-blank range doesn't leave much when the target is small. The smell of sulfur hangs onto the smoke-filled air. The cash register drawer is open. The small convenience store is empty of life and silent, but for the melancholy hum of the old fluorescent lights and the occasional bump of a night bug hitting the big front window.

"I think that ought to about do it, Dr. McFarland," he said as he handed me the document.

The mention of my name snapped me back to the present. I wasn't happy with myself for having to be brought back. It was a weakness I fully intended to correct. I turned from the window and confronted him.

"I don't think I need to read through it while you're here. Hell, you've filled out five of these to date and every one's been perfect," I said, giving the forms only a cursory examination. I put them in a folder titled "Texas Department of Corrections: Project Capital Rehabilitation: Monthly Progress Reports."

He smiled thinly and reached for his hat. The Jimmy Wayne Ellis sitting across from me was tall and very lean. He had a slight stoop to his gait. His hair was snow-white and his small dark eyes, once lifeless, seeming now to show a sign of light, were set in deep hollows behind jutting cheekbones. His complexion was oyster-gray and sort of pasty. Perspiration stains were starting to creep up his too-large collar and his half-Windsor was off to one side. His resemblance to Norman Bates came and went quickly in my mind.

"If it's all right with you, I'd like to report on the sixteenth next month. I'm supposed to give a short talk at the new prison. They want me to explain the program from an inmate's point of view."

"Sixteenth it is," I said as I marked my calendar.

He got up and we shook hands. He turned and walked to the door to my office, then turned back around.

"I near forgot. I . . . uh . . . I brought you a couple of poems," he said, and handed me two sheets of folded paper. "Maybe on the sixteenth you'll tell me if they're any good . . . that is, if you get the time, I mean . . ."

"I'll make the time," I said.

He nodded and left quietly.

I watched as the door closed behind him. I leaned back in my chair and took off my glasses. After every meeting with the man I found myself in a quandary. I couldn't shake my personal vision of the old man and his grandson. Actually, my nightmare was a composite of a dozen such senseless killings I'd been involved with over the years. After a while, they all run together. How much of the teenage, drug-addicted, illiterate Jimmy Wayne Ellis still remained in the forty-two-year-old man who just left? Twenty-four years earlier, a young Jimmy Wayne staggered into Wilson's Quick Stop just outside downtown Lufkin. He left with eighty-two dollars and all the potato chips he could carry. He left behind a shotgun and two lifeless piles of protoplasm. Less than half an hour later, the sheriff found him passed out about a block from the store. He was lying on a mound of dollar bills and potato chips. A jury took less than an hour to find him guilty of two counts of capital murder. A collective sigh of relief was heard around the state when he was sentenced to the electric chair in Huntsville.

For three years he waited to die. Then, in 1969, the United States Supreme Court ruled that Texas's death penalty was an aberration of the federal Constitution. It seemed to the high court that half the executed felons in the states of Texas and Georgia ought not to be black men if the law was fairly applied. A number of states were forced to rethink their capital punishment position, and people like Charles Manson in California and Jimmy Wayne in Texas were taken from death's door and given life sentences. He spent the next twenty years of his life looking at the world through the razor wire atop the penitentiary walls. During those years he seemed to change. He taught himself to read and write. He earned his GED and later a B.A. in sociology from the prison extension program of Sam Houston State University. He became a model prisoner and a trustee. In 1981, Jimmy Wayne Ellis came to the aid of a prison guard who had suffered a heart attack. He could have escaped, but instead, he administered CPR to the man and kept him alive until help arrived.

I first became aware of him in 1985. *Texas Monthly* published two poems he'd authored. It may well have been one of those poems that initially enticed me into the program.

When billionaire K. Brad Turrow offered to fund a radically new rehabilitation program for capital offenders, no one was surprised at Jimmy Wayne's selection to it. K. Brad Turrow became the focal point for the new Southern approach to the penal system and Jimmy Wayne became the centerpiece of the effort. The Jimmy Wayne who came under my supervision seemed to be a man of tempered character who had learned to live with and to control, if not totally exorcise, his personal demons. He'd been free for over six months and looked to embody everything the program shot for. He lived alone save for assorted dogs and cats. He worked an eight-hour day, paid his bills, attended church regularly, and even found time to work as a youth counselor for the county. With all of these things in his favor, why was it that I couldn't forget about the old man and his grandson?

"You about ready to head for the game?" The voice came from the now open office door. It was Tim Fields, the associate dean for academic affairs. It was poker night and I was his ride.

"Born ready. Come on in while I get my shit together," I replied as I placed Jimmy's file in the cabinet.

"Was that *the* Jimmy Wayne Ellis I saw leaving the building?" he asked.

"Might've been. He left a couple of minutes ago," I replied.

"My Lord, but he's a weird-looking son of a buck. Reminds me of the fella in that movie *Psycho*. . . . What was his name?" he asked as his memory strained.

"Norman Bates," I said indifferently.

"Yeah, that's the guy that stabbed Janet Leigh in the shower. It's always bothered me that they didn't show a little more of her, you know. Hell, if they remade the thing today, we'd all get to know Janet a lot better," he said, smiling.

"The only problem with that theory is that Janet Leigh is about seventy years old and I don't want to see her in the shower," I said, trying to get off the subject. I was well aware of Jimmy Wayne's horror-movie persona. That was the reason I met with him in the early evening. There were fewer students milling around.

Tim wandered over to the window and watched the sun set over Old Main.

"You know, I remember the case. I'd only been here about two years when he killed those folks. It was pitiful. An old man and a little boy. They didn't yell or fight or anything. He just cold-bloodedly blew them away," he said almost to himself.

I offered no comment.

"You're a stronger man than I am," he said without turning around. "I don't think I could help him . . . knowing what he is."

"*Was*, Timothy, *was* would seem to be the operative word here," I said, trying to sound as unemotional as possible. "The central assumption behind rehabilitation and parole is that a person can change. When that happens, what he was shouldn't be as important as what he has become."

"Right, but what are the guarantees that he's really changed? It ain't all that uncommon for a fella to fool the system, you know," he said with confidence.

4

"There are no guarantees . . . that sure enough is a fact," I said as I closed my briefcase. "But once I got away from the bureau and took time to look at the whole mess from a fresh perspective, it was clear to me that prisons don't solve problems. They exacerbate the very problems they are intended to solve . . . and at a huge cost. By the time the Turrow people came to me, I was ready to try something different," I said with a sigh.

"Well, I'll tell you what, you deep thinkers can deal with those large philosophical issues. It's pretty simple to me. If they'd have executed the son of a bitch back in sixty-six then there wouldn't be a need to worry about him now," he said firmly.

"But they didn't execute him back in sixty-six. They let him live. When they did that, the issue changed. The issue became what to do with him. All I'm saying is that I'm willing to explore the return on some other form of penal investment than this twelve-grand-a-year-per-man cost in TDC. Think about something for a minute. Texas has more men under lock and key than any other state in the whole goddamn country, but crime of all types is up. Hell, Tim, has it ever gone down? There's got to be a message in there somewhere, even for a Republican."

As my soapbox got taller, Tim started to grin at the corners. He's always enjoyed jerking my string. As a rule, I'm better at maintaining my composure. But then, it had been a long day.

"I bet you regret the day they snookered your ass into the program," he said.

"Every day," I said with total honesty.

"You might've been able to hide in academia if you hadn't gone and written that book," he said with a smile.

There was a good deal of truth in what he was saying. Having burned out in the FBI, I was looking to disappear into the small-town environment. I had a Ph.D. in constitutional law and a burning desire to simplify my life. I wrote the book as a cleansing process. It was about the last case I handled while with the bureau. It was the state's most in-

5

famous mass murder investigation. The book took off and became a national best-seller, and I became a "crime expert" in the eyes of the media.

"There are times when I regret writing *The Sands of Shame*," I said.

"Well, hell, I hear that money and fame ain't all they're cracked up to be . . . but I wouldn't take your place with Jimmy Wayne for any amount of money. The possibility that he'll backslide and kill again would bothers me to the point of ulcers," he said, looking me straight in the eyes.

"That possibility bothers me, too. But then, I'm bothered by the cost of gas, the hole in the ozone, the Moral Majority, Dan Quayle, and malice in general. I guess it's just a bothersome world, Tim. I try to deal with each bother in its place . . . but my primary therapy involves losing myself in our weekly poker games. Each and every Tuesday night I disassociate myself from reality by immersing my body and soul in the mindless shit you guys spew out. Somehow, when it's all over, I feel rested."

I aimed him in the direction of the door. We walked quietly to the car. He stood at his door and offered one last thought on the subject.

"You wanna know what chaps me about the whole Jimmy Wayne Ellis thing?" he asked.

"You want to know where the justice is for the old man and the boy," I said as I slid into the driver's seat.

"How'd you know that?" he asked.

"Lucky guess."

I spent the five-minute drive home trying to factor the victims and the rehabilitation into a formula that would eventually yield justice. My thoughts kept being interrupted by a stanza from one of Jimmy Wayne's poems.

> *The best of men have done wrong, pondered worse*
> *The worst of men have done good and pondered better*
> *Shadows in the forest are simply the whim of the sun.*
> *When will sweet death come softly to my night?*

$\bigtriangledown$

2

The Game

IT WAS A COUPLE of minutes past eight when we pulled into my driveway. Being burdened with a legendary "Felix Unger" complex, I was inspired by the thought of the poker crowd having the run of my house to make the two-mile trip from campus in record time.

My worst fears were realized as I entered the door. Case Bayhill was in the process of leaning over and spitting in the general direction of the Big Gulp cup he kept near his left foot. What seemed to me to be at least a pint of the obnoxious brown ooze missed the cup entirely and found its way onto my oak floor. No one at the table noticed the errant spittle, not that any of them would have given a damn had they noticed.

"Goddamn it, Case," I said as I tossed my briefcase on the couch, "I wish to hell you'd hit that friggin' cup every once in a while. If you've got to suck on that liquid cancer, at least spare me the thrill of having to clean the disgusting shit off my floor every Wednesday morning."

I went directly to the bar and got a Diet Coke. I took a long drink, got out my money, and settled into my customary chair.

Case looked up and faded into his best redneck, shit-eating grin. Then slowly, methodically, he rolled the plug to the left side of his face. Past experience told me that when the foul wad came to rest in the recesses of his left cheek, all present were about to get a dose of vintage Case Bayhill. It would be a monologue delivered in his painfully slow parodic exaggeration of a Texas drawl.

"Now doggone it, Fowler, how many times do I have to

tell ya that such language is unbecomin' in a college *profes-sor*. A man of your education ought not to have to stoop to vulgarity to make a point. Vulgarity is the tool of the ig-nernt." He paused long enough for another unsuccessful ballistic attempt. "Besides which, these here stains give the place a *au*thentic Western flavor. Shit, son, if this was New York, some drug-addicted fagaroo in pantyhose and Ropers would charge you a couple hunert dollars for stains of this quality. . . . He'd call 'em *am*biance."

With his monologue delivered, he sat back and smiled the smile of a man understandably satisfied with himself.

"Jesus H. Christ," I said with as much sarcasm as I could muster, "it must be flu season again. With every bout you dig out your old issues of the *Reader's Digest* and add five or six new words to your terminally anemic vocabulary. And as usual, you don't have a clue as to how to use them. The way I figure it, if you were to get real sick and lay up for maybe four weeks, you might be able to step all the way up to *People* or maybe even the *Enquirer*. One thing is for sure, however, the very thought of Nacogdoches having a literate police chief is mind-boggling."

Hob salted the mouth of his beer bottle and frowned. Case was about to offer a rebuttal when Hob semi-slammed his bottle on the table. It was obvious that he wanted the floor.

"Boys, I'm really fascinated all to hell with your bullshit, but the simple fact is, you're costing me money. Let's play poker, okay? Case, the bet's to you. Shit or get off the pot."

"Well, since you put it that way, Hob, I'll call the fifty cents and raise two dollars," Case said, still grinning.

Hob's irritation and Case's raise of two dollars generated some intensity to the moment. All eyes shifted to Charlie.

"Shoot," he said, "this hand looked pretty damn good until Case Maverick there raised two whole dollars. That turn of events does give a body pause. After all, Case don't have the balls to bluff at these stakes. Hell, two dollars Amer-ican represents almost a week's graft for a simpleminded hick sheriff." He took off his glasses and wiped them on his shirttail. "No . . . no, I think I best leave him to you, Hob,"

8

he said, throwing his hand into the center of the table. Hob ignored Charlie's warning and cast all caution to the wind. He not only called, he raised an additional two dollars. I've always seen a lot of Custer in Hob. Case was merciful and simply called the raise. He won as his small straight hammered Hob's three eights. Case's winning at cards and Hob's losing at cards were such constants that they had become something of a tradition. It wasn't really a matter of skill. Case was uncommonly lucky at cards and Hob was not. To his credit, however, Hob usually took his losses in stride. Tonight, it seemed to be rankling him more than was normal. Case was not alone in noticing Hob's less-than-festive attitude.

"Hob, you look lower than a broke-dick dog in a bitch kennel," Case said as he raked in the pot.

Hob finished his beer and went to get another one. As he walked, he explained that his mood had nothing to do with the events of the game. He was depressed at having attended a funeral earlier in the day.

Who died?" Tim asked.

"Clenny Parvis was lost to us a couple of days ago," he said solemnly.

God, how I hated that expression. We hadn't lost him. It wasn't like we were going to find him. That man was dead. Use the word. It's a perfectly good word.

"Who the hell was Kenny Parvis?" Charlie asked as he packed his pipe with tobacco that smelled like old leather.

"It's not Kenny. It's Clenny with a *C.* Anyway, you probably won't remember him. He was that old boy who showed us the good fishing spots in Pole Lake last summer," Hob clarified.

I remembered the fishing trip Hob was talking about. It was the last one the group as a whole attended. Actually, save for Case, there was not a real fisherman in the lot. We'd pack six cases of beer, a dozen packs of cards, a Zebco, and a worm. If the worm survived the trip, we were all the happier.

"Oh yeah, I remember him now," Charlie said. "Wasn't he a skinny old fart who always wore dirty overalls without a shirt? Had a funny way of talking, as I recall. Ended every sentence with a whistling sound. Two shiny silver front teeth. He sorta reminded me of Pa Kettle. Not the original, but the last one."

I was relieved that Charlie had seen fit to clarify which Pa Kettle he was talking about. After all, there's a world of difference between Percy Kilbride and Arthur Hunnicutt.

"A good man dies and leave it to a goddamn banker to remember him as a man with silver teeth," Hob said with a sneer.

Now Charlie Tunstil and Hob Bigby had been feuding for years. Hob taught economics at the college and held a well-known negative view of bankers in general. Charlie was the town's wealthiest banker and held a similar negative view of people without much money who taught economics. Though their bantering was constant, it was usually friendly. Occasionally, I had to referee. Before Charlie could launch his inevitable counterattack, I asked Hob what had been the cause of Clenny's demise.

"Heart attack. Went like that," Hob said, snapping his fingers.

Emmet Daw, a lifelong area resident, pointed out that Clenny had left behind six wives and fifteen kids. Clenny had just divorced his last wife when he went.

"Lord almighty . . . six different women married that old reprobate," Charlie blurted out without much thought. "Either those women were industrial-strength ugly or else old Clenny must have been hung like a bull."

I secretly suspected that it was the silver teeth. Such a display of oral opulence had been known to turn the head of more than one east-Texas siren.

"I don't see any humor in all of this," Hob protested. "All of them kids and wives was teary-eyed and grievin'. It really touched me," he said with alcohol-assisted sincerity.

"I make no claim to being an expert on religion," Tim said, "but I seem to recall Clenny doing some spirited cussing and drinking on that fishing trip. Now you tell me that he had six wives and a herd of kids. I guess I'd be safe in

10

assuming that old Clenny wasn't exactly the ideal Baptist role model. Unless there's been a serious reform in the Baptist church, they frown heavily on drinkin', cussin', and wife rentin'. I'll bet it was an interesting eulogy, given that Baptist preachers tend to be real flexible during the week but get real stiff-assed on Sunday."

Charlie was looking at Hob with larceny-filled eyes.

"Was . . . uh . . . old Clenny that good a friend of yours? I mean we all know how you hate funerals and all," he asked without looking at Hob.

I didn't know where he was heading, but I had a suspicion. Hob had a reputation around town as a man who liked to trifle with married women from time to time. He once told me that married women posed less of a threat to his life-style than single women. Married women, he contended, were seldom looking for long-term, meaningful relationships. They were looking for a little variety, a little spice, and a lot of friction. Those were attitudes that Hob found most attractive in a woman.

"Didn't I hear that you were squiring around Joy Lynn Reamer?" Case asked. "As I recall, she was one of Clenny's exes."

"I know the woman," Hob allowed.

"You best be extra careful. Her new husband, Clem, is a real mean son of a bitch. Real jealous, too. Now Joy Lynn, as I recall, is a little bitty thing with major hooters. I had to arrest old Clem for beatin' Wally Houk like a redheaded stepchild . . . for just admirin' them hooters. Anyone fishin' in Joy Lynn's pond best be real cautious," Case concluded with something approaching mock solemnity.

Hob considers himself a rake and he enjoys the rumors. Like most men, I think he enjoys the publicity more than the sex, which is why most get so little of both.

"The actual truth is, me and Joy Lynn are more distant friends than we used to be," he explained. "When we first met, I didn't know anything about Clem's reputation. After I got wind of it, Joy Lynn and I sort of redefined our relationship one night while Clem was working graveyard at the

11

paper mill. I hadn't seen her since then, until today that is. Clem went fishin' down at Toledo Bend. She was too sad to go to the funeral alone. I couldn't turn her down," he said with the innocent look of a cherubic, but perverted, choirboy.

"How's the crime business these days?" Emmet asked Case, having gotten bored with Hob's exploits.

"Same old, same old," he said with a bored sigh. "An occasional drunken fight, at least one woody gets out of control every month, and lately we been havin' to run high-schoolers out from behind Jiffy Lube where they been parkin' on weekends." I thought back to my own high school sexual encounters and decided that the Jiffy Lube was an amazingly appropriate place for such trysts to be conducted.

The next few minutes were abnormally quiet as everyone concentrated on their cards. The minimized patter paid off for Case. He won most of those hands, too.

From out in left field, Case changed the subject.

"I have it from reliable sources that old Fowler has been offered not one, but two new jobs," he said quietly, avoiding direct eye contact with me.

"Where in the hell did you come up with that?" I asked.

"My sources are confidential. The Angelina School of Law Enforcement was very clear about keeping good sources confidential. Let's just say that I was forced to use the most sophisticated methods of information extractin'."

"Well, hell, you're the man with all the information." I implored him to continue with a wave of my hands.

"As I hear it, you was offered a teaching job at SMU and you got an offer from a Hollywood-type company to write a movie version of your book. I hear that you turned 'em both down," he said as he tried to read my reaction.

"Fowler," Fields said emphatically, "if you turned down a job at SMU and a job in Hollywood to teach at a piss-ant college like Stephen F. Austin in a chickenshit town like this, son, you're legally dead in this state. Folks are being committed for making better decisions than that one."

It was a constant source of bewilderment to people in Nacogdoches that anyone would leave big-city success to live in a small town. I had always thought it interesting that a lot of people living in large cities longed for the simplicity they thought was endemic to all small towns. On the other side of the coin were the hordes of small-towners who longed for the glitz and excitement of bright lights and endless opportunity.

"I've got enough money and I'm comfortable with my life. Dallas and SMU offer nothing that I want. I know that you boys see something special in Dallas. To me it's simply the largest concentration of Republican arrogance in the state. As for Hollywood, old Case's reliable sources were a mite off. They offered me a lot of money to take a year off and go out there and write a screenplay for *The Sands of Shame*. I told them no. We're still talking about my possibly writing the screenplay from here." I hoped that the subject would fade quickly.

"I expect there's got to be some serious money in writing one of them movie scripts," Emmet half asked and half asserted.

Charlie took on an uncomfortable look. It was either serious gas from the jalapeño dip or a negative reaction to my cavalier attitude toward money. Money occupied a special place in his heart. I decided that the pained expression was probably born of dual causality.

"The way I figure it, there's only one reason why a man would turn down more money—hell, come to think on it, more of everything—to stay here," Emmet said confidently. There was silence as everyone waited with bated breath for the conclusion of this latest Dawism. Emmet was known for his ability to spray a room with malapropisms. He once referred to T. Boone Pickens as T. Bone Pickens and on another occasion substituted IOU for IUD in a conversation on birth control.

"The truth is that Fowler can't stand the thought of leaving all the college quaff behind," he announced with an air of finality in his tone.

Case broke into a broad smile. Charlie looked confused. Tim just sat there mumbling under his breath.

"Someone want to educate an ignorant country boy? What the hell is *quaff*?" Charlie asked.

"I'm not absolutely sure, but I think that *quaff* is supposed to be *quiff*. I believe it's a matter of Emmet confusing his chauvinistic crudities. In the attempt to pronounce cheap detective-novel vernacular, he is implying that I am loyal to SFA because of the availability of willing coeds," I explained delicately.

Hob looked almost blissful.

"Quiff . . . quiff . . . I love the sound of it. It has such a wholesome ring to it. Romantic, you know. Sounds a little like a dairy product . . . cheese quiff . . . whipped quiff . . . chilled quiff. Son of a bitch, there are some sweet possibilities in there," he proclaimed while in the throes of a full body shiver.

I was about to suggest that Hob contact the American Dairy Association and offer his suggestion for a possible new product line. I even had a slogan prepared for the national ad campaign: "Quiff, the low-calorie spread with just the right aftertaste." But before I could capitalize on the moment the phone rang.

Phone calls this late in the game usually meant one of two things. Either Emmet's wife, Pearlene, was checking on him again, or the police dispatcher, Arlo Pirtle, had a problem that required Case's personal attention.

The deep, thick drawl immediately told me it was Arlo. It wasn't deep enough to be Pearlene. I called Case to the phone. If it followed form, Case would listen patiently for a few seconds, then explain what was always fairly commonsensical to begin with.

I watched Case out of the corner of my eye. Curiously, it was taking longer than usual. I could see Case stiffen up. I couldn't make out any of the conversation, but his tone and posture told me that something wasn't right. He hung up the phone and stood there for a few seconds, collecting his thoughts. He took a deep breath and came back to the table.

"There's been a killin'. I best be gettin' on over there," he said quietly as he took his hat and gun from the hearth.

14

Killings aren't everyday occurrences in Nacogdoches. There was a brief moment of stunned silence. A chorus of questions quickly followed.

"Look, fellas," he said as he missed the damned cup for the umpteenth time, "I don't know a hell of a lot."

"Who got killed? Emmet asked.

"Don't have a for-sure name yet. It's a woman. She lived in a duplex over in the Tallow Creek subdivision off north two-fifty-nine," he said, turning toward the front door.

I walked with him to the door.

"Stay near the phone, will ya?" he said quietly. "I can't afford another Beayne Congrady on my record."

"All right."

The news of the killing dampened the enthusiasm for serious gambling. In spite of my best efforts, it proved impossible to get their minds back on track. After an hour or so, I gave in to their banal curiosity and told them to go home.

I went outside to unwind on the deck. The phone brought me back inside.

"How's the game goin'?" the voice asked.

"It isn't," I answered. "Broke up about twenty minutes ago."

"This looks pretty nasty. I'd feel better if you'd come on over and take a look." His voice was tired.

"What's the address?"

"Twenty-two-eleven Tallow Lane. Apartment of a Maureen Wilson. You know how to get here?"

"Yeah, I can find it. You sound a little edgy," I added.

"Well shit-fire, Fowler, what do I have to be edgy about? I got one dead woman, I got one unsolved murder already draggin' my ass down, I got an election comin' up, and it looks like I may be unemployed. Other than that, I ain't got any fuckin' worries at all," he snapped.

"I'm on my way."

In the summer, east Texas is hot and humid during the day and still hot and humid at night. This was a typical August night. There wasn't a hint of breeze and the damp

15

air set heavy on your skin. I put the top down and headed for the other side of town. Once I was moving, the night air became bearable. I pushed in a sixties tape and looked for a convenience store. It was clear to me that this night was going to require a lot of caffeine.

As impossible as it may seem, I didn't pass a single convenience store. I made a mental note to contact the Ripley people in the morning. It took less than ten minutes to locate the neighborhood. As I pulled onto Tallow Lane, Elvis had just discovered that Marie was the name of his best friend's latest flame. I knew there wouldn't be a problem finding the duplex because the location would undoubtedly be marked by the presence of every police vehicle within a thirty-mile radius. They would all have their lights flashing and their radios blaring. They would be awkwardly parked so that normal traffic flow would be impossible. Such a scene makes for good television drama, but reflects idiot-level police training. The excitement generated by the cop avalanche would attract every living organism to the crime scene. How smart do you have to be to understand that the larger the number of people tramping around, the greater the likelihood that evidence will be ruined? The Angelina School of Law Enforcement at work.

I parked a couple of houses down the street and walked toward the organized chaos.

"That was fast," Case said, looking at his watch.

I nodded silently. I found myself immersed in the activity around me. It was scenes like this that had led to my leaving the bureau for the classroom. It was a strange feeling to hate everything about what was going on, but be compelled to participate. My life was real clear right now, but there were shadows here.

"You look a mite puny, boy. Somethin' wrong?" he asked.

I counted over a half-dozen jurisdictions wandering aimlessly around. Any other time, a person would have to go to a Dunkin' Donuts to find that many cops.

"Looks to me like you've got enough help around here. It's been a lot of years. Hell, Case, I doubt I can add anything to

16

what you already know," I said with little enthusiasm.

"Is that right?" he said as he pushed his hat back and steered me in the direction of the garage. We took a position behind a large cedar tree outside of easy view from the house.

"Why don't you just kiss my tight white ass, but while you're puckerin' up, spare me the horseshit will ya please," he said in a poorly regulated attempt at whispering, which frequently lapsed into a near yell. He paused and spit into the roses. "It's been a lot of years . . . my happy ass. You were the best damn federal cop in the whole fuckin' country. A regular bluetick hound, to hear Kermit Greenburg tell it. And we both know a man don't forget what he's best at."

I didn't say anything. I just thought about the situation.

"Aw, hell, Fowler, I ain't got the crime of the century here. But I just can't afford any loose ends right now. I'm a pretty good cop, but I need an edge, and the only edge I got is you."

While he talked, I surveyed the area. I'd decided a couple of minutes earlier to help him. I just hadn't gotten around to telling him yet.

"You owe me this one," he said with conviction.

I gave him my "how-do-you-figure-it" look.

"For starters, if it hadn't been for me, Ed Andy would've killed you that night at Beefy's—and you damn well know I'm tellin' you the truth. Plus, I'm the only living witness to the time you fried your dick on old man Cooperman's hot wire," he said, pausing long enough to spit. The pause gave me time enough to remember those blue flames shooting upstream with my manhood as their final destination. The sight of my smoking genitals is forever with me. Mercifully, he interrupted the flashback.

"I swear to almighty God, Fowler, if you back out on me now, I'll never back up your story again."

For the first time, I understood the look on Milburn Stone's face all those years when he was confronted by the convoluted logic of Ken Curtis. All I could do was shake my head and walk toward the house.

I stopped short of the door.

"The first thing you need to do is clear the entire area of

17

anyone who doesn't have a purpose for being here. Most of these cops are just curious. There's no reason for them to roam around and maybe mess up some evidence." I was talking as quietly as I could so as not to give the impression that Case wasn't calling the shots.

"Anything else?" he asked.

"I'd cordon off the entire area, including the other rental unit. You might want to put up the other renter at the Holiday Inn for a couple of nights. . . . Oh yeah, you might want to cordon off that wooded lot over there," I said, pointing to a vacant lot that bordered the duplex on the left.

"Where's the body?" I asked.

$\triangledown$

3

Death in Nacogdoches

IT'S DIFFICULT TO DESCRIBE the feeling of a room where a murder has taken place. There's a sort of lingering energy present. Maybe it's a residue left over from the act itself. I'm not especially religious and I don't believe in the supernatural, military intelligence, or coed virginity. I can't rationally explain it, but it's there. I'd felt it often and I felt it now.

Case had cleared the room to allow me some privacy. He assured me that everything in the room was as it had been when his men first arrived. Even the body was largely undisturbed. It had been examined only by a paramedic team. The coroner, an old classmate of ours, Bobby Joe Hogedon, hadn't made it yet. He hadn't been located until a few minutes before when he was uncovered at a motel in Crocket doing some after-hours anatomy research. I figured I had about an hour before he could get here. All things considered, that was a lucky break. Bobby Joe had demonstrated a greater talent for examining live bodies than dead ones.

I found a spot that supplied me with the best overall view of the room. I sat on the floor near the door to the hall, and took my time as I surveyed the entire room carefully. I wanted a complete mental picture of the scene. I wanted to visualize the most probable scenario given the logistics of the room.

It was the bedroom of a single woman with definite tastes. Everything was feminine in the traditional sense. The walls were done in peach, or maybe apricot. I always get the two confused. In any case, the walls were some off-shade of pink. The curtains, bedspread, and reading chair were all of a matching floral pattern. On one wall there were several pictures. They had an old, rustic look about them. Judging from the fashion of the day, I guessed that these pictures were a couple of decades old. Hanging over the bed was a large picture of Jesus with its own small light attached to the top of the frame. I'd seen enough from my initial vantage point. I got up and started to move slowly around the room.

The dresser top was cluttered with mementos and female paraphernalia. There was a hairbrush, a box of curlers, a bowling trophy for high series, an inexpensive music box, a stack of travel brochures, and a copy of the 1954 Tyler High School yearbook. I flipped through the pages of the yearbook. I've always loved these things. This one was a little on the sad side. There were only six signatures and inscriptions. That's not many to show for four years of your life.

The closet revealed an inexpensive wardrobe consisting mostly of cotton and polyester clothes of the Weiner's variety. Not many shoes for a woman. With the exception of a sixteen-pound bowling ball, there wasn't a masculine object in the room.

The dead woman was lying faceup on the bed. She was naked but for a sock on her left foot. A bra was tightly wound around her neck. It had been so tightly twisted that the shoulder straps had cut into her neck, which was swollen and badly bruised. Her eyes were bulging and the facial expression was one I'd seen before. There was little doubt that the woman had died from strangulation.

The bed was made, but mussed. Actually, there were damn few signs of a struggle. The furniture was in place and the dresser items weren't all that chaotic. Judging from the degree of rigor, she had been dead for three or four hours at most. There wasn't any evidence of blood or tissue under her fingernails.

Given the position of the body, rape seemed probable. She was spread-eagled across the bed and her breasts showed signs of discoloration. Interestingly, I could find no traces of blood or seminal fluid. That's fairly unusual in what appears to be a violent rape. Forced penetration usually causes some vaginal damage and that's normally indicated by the presence of some bleeding.

20

She was wearing a cocktail ring on her right hand. Her Timex was still on her wrist. Neither appeared to be especially valuable.

Her clothes were torn and strewn about. Her pale pink blouse had evidently been ripped from her body. The clasp on her pants was broken and the zipper was off the track. Both garments were at the foot of her bed. Her tattered panties were dangling from the bedpost. They reminded me of a battle-scarred flag.

The only outside entry to the room was through a window. It opened to the backyard. It was securely locked, and I found no indication of forced entry. The killer had to have entered the house in another room. I decided to check the other bedroom. It, too, had one window. The latch was in place, but there were faint scratches around it. A small spiderweb was broken and hanging in the upper-right corner of the window.

The rest of the house consisted of a living area, a small kitchen, and a single bathroom. I went through each of the rooms looking for anything out of place. All the usual items that a burglar might take were undisturbed and visible. In the rear of the kitchen was a washer and dryer. I looked at the small pile of dirty clothes on top of the dryer.

I examined the outer doors and found nothing to suggest forced entry. I went back to the bedroom and looked through her drawers. I must be slipping. Looking in those drawers should've been automatic. When I closed the last drawer, I knew it was time to talk to Case. He was conducting a search of the exterior. I could hear his voice in the darkness and could make out about a dozen flashlights moving around the yard. Case must've spotted me, because he suddenly appeared in the light. We started to amble toward my car.

"Tell me somethin' I don't know," he said.

"Does it look like rain to you?" I asked.

"No, it don't," he answered as he looked heavenward.

"Then why not close up shop for the night. It's even money you ruin as much evidence as you find in the dark. Need good light to do it right," I explained as one of his people stumbled and fell over a hose. He landed awkwardly in the flower bed. "Why don't I meet you about nine tomorrow morning? Meantime, why don't you post a couple of men here for the night. Tell them to pick highly visible spots and stay put. Their goal is simply to keep the curious and the morbid away. It's particularly important that one of your people keep everyone away from that wooded lot over there," I said, pointing.

Case followed my finger with his eyes. "Want to tell me what's so goddamn important about that lot?" he asked.

"Just covering all the possibilities," I said without further explanation. "When your men arrived, were the doors locked from the inside?"

"The back door was locked and bolted from the inside. The front door was locked but the deadbolt wasn't in," he said.

"Anyone around here hear anything at all?" I asked.

"Not so far. The woman who lives in the other unit was here until eight-thirty. Says she went to Lumberjack's for a beer. Didn't hear nothin' unusual and really didn't know the woman that well. By the way, the neighbor is a good lookin' coed type," he said as he put his little notebook away and bit off another plug.

We stopped at the end of the driveway and leaned against a patrol car.

"Who reported the murder?" I asked.

Out came the notebook again. "We got a call from a Helen Burris about ten o'clock. She'd been playin' cards with the deceased until about eight-fifteen. Miss Wilson complained of a fever and left for home. The Burris woman came by to borrow a dress. Miss Wilson was expectin' her to drop by. When she got there, the lights were on, but no one answered the door. She found her car in the garage and called us. That's all she knew," he concluded, and put the notebook away again.

His notebook had always tickled me. I'm sure that he picked it up from watching old episodes of *Columbo*. He had been addicted to the program for years. He never missed a

22

rerun and knew most of the dialogue by heart. Case was a combination of Gomer Pyle and Columbo. A sort of Gomer Columbo.

Suddenly I was aware of the mosquitoes. Around here, when these bastards start to loot and pillage, it's time for the prudent to seek shelter. The clothes were also starting to stick to my body. I needed a cold Coke, an air-conditioned room, and some sleep. I started to head to my car. Case looked confused.

"You ain't plannin' on leavin' here without tellin' me somethin' are you?" he asked with the beginnings of a peeved look on his face. He started to spit.

"I wouldn't spit around here if I were you," I said.

He looked disgusted. I think he was suspicious of my motives where the subject of his chewing was concerned.

"Why the shit not?" he asked.

"Well it just might be that our killer is as ignorant as you are about oral cancer. Wouldn't it be nice if any stains we find tomorrow were his. We might get lucky and be able to trace 'em and get a lead."

He shook his head slightly, mumbled something inaudible, spit in his hand, and walked off.

I was surprised that he had given up on questioning me so easily. He must have been real tired. I took the long way home. There was a 7-Eleven along this route. I was in dire need of caffeine and something cold.

Forty-four ounces of caffeine combined with a large dose of curiosity can make for a relatively sleepless night.

The next morning I was wired. All the juices were flowing. I was uncomfortably eager to get on with this.

Case was standing next to his car when I drove up. He looked like shit warmed over. His eyes were a rich red and he looked as if he hadn't slept a wink.

"How's it hanging, Fowler?" he asked.

"Too early to tell, but I expect to make it," I answered. "And you?"

"Don't ask," he responded.

23

"Got anything new on the dead woman?"

"Not much to speak about. We got verification of her identity. She was fifty-six and single. Never been married and lived alone. She was an English teacher at the high school. Pretty much your basic spinster."

"Was the card game a regular affair?" I asked.

"Same group of women played hearts every Tuesday night. They rotated the host house."

"What about the forensics?" I asked.

"Bobby Joe told me this morning that the stuff relatin' to the cause of death and the rape will be available later this evening or early tomorrow. Crime scene evidence will take a little longer. Hell, we got about a dozen different sets of prints from around the house. We're tryin' to print everyone who had a legitimate reason to be there. Maybe we'll come up with a set of prints that don't belong," he said.

As we talked, I had us moving in the direction of the guest bedroom window. When we got there I pointed to the minute scratches around the latch. I explained the technique used by good burglars. He pointed out that those scratches could've gotten there in a lot of ways other than a break-in. I didn't pursue the point, and I didn't point out the spider-web he didn't notice.

We left the window and walked to the wooded lot east of the house.

"What are we lookin' for?" Case asked as we walked.

"Right now we're looking for the spot in these trees that has the clearest view of the duplex," I answered.

About fifty yards from the house we found an area in a small grove of tallow and pine. The grass was beaten down. It was obvious that someone had recently spent some time there. Whoever it was had left nothing save for three cigarette butts. Not being a smoker, I'm not real familiar with tobacco products. I do, however, have a very well developed sense of smell. My dad used to say that I could smell a gnat fart at a hundred yards. My dad exaggerated some. I figured fifty yards tops. These butts had a peculiar smell about them. I dislike the smell of most cigarettes and cigars. But these little devils

24

had a distinctive, sweet aroma. Even a night in the humidity hadn't dulled the odor. There was a second, less pungent smell that reminded me of pears. Case took two of the little brown stubs and put them in an evidence bag. I talked him into loaning me the third one. I planned to take it over to Homer. He owned the town's only real tobacco shop. We prowled around for a few more minutes and came up empty. The ground was too hard to yield any prints.

The wooded lot was actually four undeveloped lots. It was bordered on three sides by residential streets with tract housing of the sort that characterizes lower-middle-income neighborhoods in the area. Case and I carefully walked the street frontage. There were no tire tracks leading into the lot. No sign of a vehicle of any type driving into the woods. Either our man had parked his car somewhere else and walked into the lot or he had been dropped off and picked up.

"Case, you need to find out if anyone saw a car or a truck parked anywhere along this route last night," I suggested.

He nodded and wrote in the notebook.

Before leaving the area I leaned up against the most comfortable of the trees and discovered that, from that vantage point, I could see the side of Miss Wilson's unit and the backs of both units. Anyone coming from the garage to the back door would be visible. I knew all I was going to know until I saw the forensics reports.

We went to my car.

Case looked mad enough to punch a nun. "Now hold your goddamn horses here," he commanded. "Don't be gettin' me out here this mornin', runnin' me around, and then haulin' ass without tellin' me nothin' I can use." He spit in his can. "I ain't ever enjoyed being wet, ready, and alone. I'm pickin' up a strange smell here. You best explain it some."

"I've got a few ideas, but I need the forensics reports before I talk about them. Let's have dinner at Tommy's about six. You bring the lab reports and whatever your men are able to find out about vehicles in the area, and we'll talk it over," I said, indifferent to his aggressive impatience. "Oh, as for the

25

smell, don't worry about it. It's probably just the inside of your mouth starting to rot and decay."

"You got a real mean streak in you, you know that?" he asked.

I started her up. "No one's ever mentioned it before . . . Wensel." I drove off knowing the scowl he would assume having heard his hated name. No one ever spoke it around him. Well, almost no one. Occasionally I felt the need to use it for humbling purposes.

I wondered how Case was going to react to what I was probably going to have to say.

Homer Mangum is one of the most interesting men I've ever known. He made a fortune in insurance in Dallas. About five years ago he retired from the business and moved to Nacogdoches. He immediately opened a bookstore followed by a tobacco shop. Both are more hobbies than businesses. He's fifty-six years old and perhaps the best read and most polished man in town. He loves exotic tobaccos and expensive pipes. His shop caters to those with discerning tastes. He shelves no Skoal or Kodiak. He can usually be found reading a book with one of his meerschaums in full flower. We had always gotten on famously, as he liked to put it.

"Good morning, Fowler. And what brings you into my world this fine morning?" he asked. Homer is a slight man who had always reminded me of Barry Fitzgerald.

"Hello, Homer. I've come to you with a bit of intrigue that I thought you might help me with," I said.

He peered at me over his half-glasses. He marked his place and set the book on the table.

"It wouldn't have anything to do with the murder last night, would it?" he asked with anticipation.

"It's entirely possible," I said. "I need to know something about this." I handed him the butt still in the plastic bag.

He took a pair of tweezers from a drawer. He extracted the butt and held it to his nose. He then held it to the light of the window. He placed it back in the bag and returned it to me.

26

"What we have here is a real high-ticket item. It's a hand-made, international mixture of expensive leaves. It's not a shelf sitter. Probably specially made for a select few customers."

"Where would I be able to get one of these?" I asked.

Homer smiled. "It would be an expensive proposition. The cigarettes would cost about a dollar apiece. The real cost would be in getting to the East Coast where you could find them. I doubt that they could be found in Dallas or Houston," he said with confidence.

"Would it be possible to trace this cigarette to a specific shop on the East Coast?" I asked.

"Possibly, but it would be a real long shot. The paper is an expensive but not uncommon stock. The leaves are available in many shops. There is no trademark on the butt. I wouldn't take the bet at any odds," he said.

"Homer . . . I'd appreciate it if this conversation were to stay just between us," I said.

"What conversation is that?" he asked rhetorically as he reopened his book.

In all probability, Homer had just provided me with confirmation for a disturbing theory that had been taking form since the previous night.

I glanced at my watch. It was almost one o'clock. I had just enough time to make the lecture. I pushed in a tape and headed to the campus.

4

Beth

I FOUND A NOTE on the door. It was from a past student, Elizabeth Sue Bush. I hadn't seen her in a couple of semesters. She should have been just about finished with her master's degree, I thought. Several things about Beth came to mind. She was bright, aggressive, and sensual. She had taken two classes with me. Toward the end of the second one, I got the impression that she was interested in escalating our relationship beyond student and teacher. It wasn't anything she said as much as a series of subtle looks and intonations. Unfortunately I have two steadfast rules about that. The first is that I don't pursue or bed a student of mine. I also avoid the infirm, the deceased, and the ugly. I consider all other women to be fair game. The second rule concerns interpreting the intentions of women. I don't. The male ego, self-serving as it is, will always assume female intentions are sexual.

The note said that she'd stop back later. Two additional thoughts came to mind with respect to Beth. She was no longer a student of mine. Nor was she likely to be again. Second, she was endowed with possibly the finest ass in the Western Hemisphere.

I usually avoid teaching in the summer. I use the time to drive around the country, which I like to do, and regenerate my professional batteries, which I need to do. This summer I had decided to stay home and work on some writing I'd been putting off. As a favor to a friend, I volunteered to guest lecture in one of his classes for the week of his honeymoon.

Actually I was enjoying the class. It was titled "Contemporary Issues in Journalism." This week we were discussing

28

the concept of ethics in the print media. It had been fun so far. The class was enthusiastic and aggressive. Today we were discussing the implications of a recent Virginia court decision that held that a nationally circulated men's magazine, which handily doubles as a gynecology journal, had to pay two hundred thousand dollars in damages to a nationally known television evangelist because he supposedly suffered severe anguish as a result of an article in the magazine. Personally, I find the magazine to be vulgar and tasteless. With good cause, I don't care if it's sued out of existence. However, in my opinion, this suit lacked good cause. The thing that bothered me about this particular decision was that the court ruled that the damages should be awarded even though, legally speaking, no libel was proven. The result of the decision appeared to be that First Amendment parameters were irrelevant in libel cases. All a person had to do to collect damages was show that they were upset with the article. Malice and intent were no longer essential to the case.

Should this ruling stand, the primary goal of the press would shift from reporting the news to being inoffensive. It would emasculate the First Amendment.

When I walked in the door, the eager young minds were poised and ready for the discussion. Anyone doubting that the sixties are gone forever, be forewarned. I was mortified to discover that damn near none of them saw any reason for alarm in the ruling. It was a scary moment when I realized I was alone and unarmed in front of so many larva-stage Republicans. While they weren't mature killing machines yet, it was obvious that philosophically, they were well on their way.

It soon became clear that a young man named Norman Fuqua had assumed the role of spokesman for those who felt compelled to assassinate the First Amendment. I asked him to encapsulate the position of his flock.

"Well, Dr. McFarland . . . the article in question is actually a series of cartoons. They depict the pastor and members of his family as being involved in bestiality and incest. These depictions were utterly disgusting and served no journalistic purpose at all. They served only to inflict pain and anguish on a man of God and his family." He paused and looked around the room. "Frankly, sir, I think the court decision simply reflects the consensus position in the country that we will no longer tolerate filthy rags hiding behind the Constitution." With a sickening smile on his always pleasant face, he sat down.

The young man was lost to journalism. If there ever was a genetic evangelist, it was Norman.

I held out hope, faint as it was, that someone would rise up and defend the Constitution and the profession to which they all aspired. For want of an advocate, I was about to reluctantly champion the cause myself when I heard a female voice from behind me. As the discussion progressed, I had moved around the room and eventually settled with my back to the door. Unknown to me at the time, a visitor had made her way into our midst. We often had visitors, but they weren't usually this vocal. I immediately recognized the earthy voice with the slight Southern flavor.

"Dr. McFarland, I'm not a paying customer in this class, so if you or anyone else would prefer it, I'll be quiet," Beth said.

"Miss Bush, the comments of an outstanding graduate student are always welcome," I said.

"I find this decision to be a truly pitiful example of legal reasoning. Should it stand, and I'm sure it won't, it would deal a crippling blow to freedom of expression in general and to journalism in particular. Those defending the decision are on dangerous footing."

I was glad to see that Beth hadn't developed any tact since our last discussion.

"The article," she continued, "is a cartoon parody, not a news story. Satire is offensive by design. If it doesn't smart a little, it isn't satire. It draws its essence from sarcasm." She stopped long enough to allow rebuttal if any were in the offing. She scanned the room. None was.

"The statement that offended me most in all of this was the one about public consensus. It has always been my understanding that the Constitution is amendable only through process and not by Gallup poll. The law is real clear with respect to what constitutes libel. Heretofore, you were either guilty of libel or you weren't. If you were guilty, then you paid damages. If you weren't guilty, then you didn't pay damages. This decision takes a relatively simple concept and renders it incomprehensible," she concluded.

The class just sat there mute.

"Well, ladies and gentlemen of the fifth estate, I suggest you spend some time this evening considering the issue of the day. We'll pick up here tomorrow. Until then, try to find someone comfortable and afflict them," I said as they exited.

Beth and I made our way out of the room.

"It's good to see you. Have you time to drop by my office and talk?" Beth walked in front of me. I was delighted to see that some things never change.

The phone was ringing as we opened the door. It was Cora Slick, the department secretary. She was one of my ten favorite people. She had a mouth like a sailor and a kick-ass, take-no-prisoners personality. She's also the best damned secretary I've ever worked with.

"Fowler, you've got two important messages. I promised both men I'd talk to you personally. Boyd Fuchs called about some letter you wrote for the mayor." She always mispronounced his last name. "He didn't sound happy. Wanted me to make sure you called him immediately . . . what a numbnuts. Case Bayhill called and said that he'd be in his office after four-thirty. Who won all the money last night?" she asked.

"Case did about all the winning that took place. The killing cut the game a little short . . . Cora, do me a favor. I've got a friend in my office at the moment. Call Fuchs for me and tell him that if he wants to meet with me, it'll have to be at five o'clock today, or it'll have to wait until tomorrow. Get back to me on that, will you? I'll call Case myself."

"Fowler, you really think that the Wilson woman was raped and killed by some hitchhikin' Mexican?" she asked.

"I have my doubts about that. Why? You got some reason why that boat won't float?" I asked without inquiring about the origin of that particular theory.

31

"Shit-fire, have you seen the Wilson woman? We're talking ugly taken to a new dimension. All I can say is this couldn't have been a crime of passion, if you know what I mean," Cora said unequivocally.

"I'll be sure and pass that theory on to Case when I talk to him later," I said.

"Keep it hard, Fowler," she said as she hung up.

I told Beth that I needed to call the police chief about a recent killing. She got up and walked to the bookcases on the far wall and did some browsing among the volumes. As I dialed, I watched her move around. Beth was five four or five five and weighed about a hundred pounds or so. Her hair was chestnut and her brown eyes mischievous. Some women work at looking sexy, some don't have to. Beth was in the latter category. She gave off sparks and was as close to pure high-octane estrogen as anyone I'd ever encountered. She was also bright and playful. I've always thought that a really bright, sexy woman might be the most dangerous creature on this planet. What the hell, you got to die from something.

Case's secretary, Annie, put me right through.

"Fowler, I got most of the reports. They're preliminary, but hell, the final results don't usually change much. You want to meet me somewhere and go over 'em?" he asked.

My curiosity about these reports was barely stronger than my libido.

"Hit me with the high points now and we'll have dinner at Tommy's and go into more detail," I said.

"Okay . . . let's see here. The cause of death was strangulation. Time of death was about nine P.M. Her windpipe was crushed. She was choked from the rear by a lefty. Says here that there was evidence of sexual penetration. Probably forced."

"Case, there wasn't any evidence of semen, was there?"

"No . . . there wasn't. . . . How the hell did you know that?" he asked back. Before I had an opportunity to comment, he continued. "I figure the guy was either fixed or just couldn't get off all the way. You know some of these perverts ain't normal."

It was a theory not worthy of comment, so I didn't.

"Did anyone see a car parked in the area we talked about?" I asked.

"There weren't no cars there that night. Two local guys jog that street every night between eight and ten. They claimed to have stopped and rested on the curb right in front of the wooded lot. They both were sure that no vehicle of any type was parked in the area."

Beth was making no pretense of polite indifference with respect to the conversation.

"What about fingerprints?" I asked.

"We found two sets of prints we can't account for yet," he replied. "But we haven't run down everyone with normal access to the house. Right now we don't know if we have the killer's prints or not."

"Where'd you lift the prints?"

"Let's see . . . one was in the guest bathroom on the toilet seat. The other was on a glass in the kitchen. Why?" he asked.

I replied with controlled impatience. "Case, if you were a killer clever enough to break into the house with the skill of a cat burglar, kill and rape the woman without being seen or heard, would you then be stupid enough to get a drink and forget to wipe your prints? Or better still, take a piss and raise and lower the seat politely? And, of course, forget to wipe your prints again? Not likely. One of two things is true about the prints. Either the killer is someone with normal access to the house, in which case you have his prints and don't know it. Or none of the prints found in the house belong to the killer because he was either gloved or careful."

"Shit, boy, it sounds to me like you givin' a load of credit to this ol' boy. What's not to say that this feller was just passin' through and stopped to have a smoke. Took a peek in the bedroom window. Got tired of window shoppin' and gave the window a little jerk and it came open. The woman was in another room and didn't hear the noise. He banged her brains out, panicked a little, and killed her," he concluded with conviction.

"That the way you see it?" I asked.

"It makes more sense than makin' him out to be some sort of master criminal," he said.

This wasn't the time or place to compare theories with Case. His present theory had about as much reason to it as a Ronald Reagan impromptu answer. It wasn't that he was incapable of reason. Case simply tended to be a mite visceral from time to time. Besides, my libido was overpowering my curiosity.

"I'll tell you what, after you buy my dinner I'll compare theories with you," I offered.

"If you want the city to fork over any eatin' money, you better come up with some heavy-duty information," he countered.

"Scotland Yard wouldn't treat Holmes that way," I protested.

"I don't know what all that bullshit means, but you're goin' to have to be extra smart to eat free. See you about seven o'clock," he said and hung up.

No sooner had I put the receiver down than it rang again.

"Fowler, Dean Fuchs would like to see you in his office in fifteen minutes," Cora said with mock formality.

Beth had listened to the conversations and surmised a good deal.

"This is not a good time for us to talk, is it?" she asked.

"Not right this minute, but I'd like to get together later if you've the time," I said.

She gave me a strange look. It was as if she was carefully considering her next comment.

"The main reason I'm in Nacogdoches is to see you. I'm free until tomorrow sometime," she said without blinking or stuttering.

"How about eight o'clock at Tommy's?" I asked.

She walked to the door, turned, and smiled. "That works for me," she said as she closed the door.

It occurred to me that the priority status of this killing was slipping with me. Case wasn't getting a minute of my time past eight.

5

The Peter Principle

I REALLY DISLIKE FUCHS. But I don't like the fact that I dislike him. Any intense emotion seems to me to extend value to him. For several years I had been successful in avoiding him. Then a couple of months ago he was promoted to the position of dean of public affairs. It's a position that forces occasional contact. As an administrator, he incarnates everything I find undesirable in administration. That's understandable, I guess, when you realize that, as a human being, he's a popcorn fart.

He is a dean by association. He didn't prepare himself for the position in any professional way. Boyd simply kissed enough of the right ass to move from the classroom to the ivory tower. He's a fake good old boy who has fallen in with the right, if gullible, good old boys. He's the embodiment of the "Peter Principle." Not only has he risen to his level of incompetence, but he also is a peter in every sense of the word.

His most endearing quality is his megalomania. He has a sign on his office wall that argues that those who don't use their power lose it. Given that philosophy, is it any wonder that he was adored by faculty and staff alike?

When I got to his office, I was somewhat surprised to find him in the company of Nacogdoches's esteemed mayor, Ed Andy Andrews. Now this was an interesting duo to be sure. Aside from being intellectual equals, they shared a dislike for me. I wasn't entirely certain what they wanted with me, but I was pretty sure it wasn't to spit, drink, and swap lies.

Boyd, preoccupied with something he was reading, barely glanced up. Ed Andy had a look on his face like someone who'd just swallowed a load of Pepto-Bismol. I took the nearest chair.

Fuchs finally looked up. It was then that I noted the silly-looking bandage he had on his nose. I thought I recalled seeing our president, Sumner Brightal, walking funny yesterday, as though he had a cob up his ass. I figure he'd been walking someplace real fast and stopped quickly. Fuchs, following in his operational position, failed to stop in time and shoved his nose halfway up Brightal's ass. Granted it was supposition, but it surely did fit all the facts.

"Fowler, we've got a problem that's entirely of *your* doing. The mayor is very upset with the college in general and with you specifically. He tells me that you have taken a flippant attitude with regard to an important public relations project for the city." He spoke with relish in his voice. He liked the idea of calling me on the carpet. I kept staring at the bandage.

"Hellfire, get on with it, Boyd," interrupted Ed Andy. "That goddamn letter you wrote is pure horseshit. But I wasn't surprised. It's the kind of shit a smart-assed, liberal college professor would write. I was against you bein' involved in this to begin with. As far as I'm concerned you ain't nothin' but a humanist prick," he concluded with a heavy dose of vocal hostility.

I pointed out to Ed that he had omitted agnostic and communist. They were usually critical elements in his descriptive monologues about me. I was impressed with one thing he said. If the letter offended him, it meant that he had both read and understood it. That would make the first time in the thirty or so years that I had known Ed Andy that he had been involved in a successful cognitive experience.

"Look," I said stoically, "I told President Brightal that ignoring the newspaper article was the best path to take. He told me that the chamber of commerce was adamant about a rebuttal. I didn't go to him and ask for the job of composing that rebuttal. He came to me. He told me to tell the truth and not to mince words. I told the truth and didn't mince words."

A couple of months back, a Little Rock newspaper had

run a story which said that nothing resembling culture could be found between Little Rock and Houston. The area in between was described as a pleasantly landscaped aesthetic wasteland. The locals became enraged and demanded a letter of rebuttal. Reluctantly, and at the president's behest, I tended to the task.

I argued that the offending article contained two obvious flaws. First, there was the eminently questionable assertion that something akin to culture can be found in either Little Rock or Houston. Second, those responsible for the original article had certainly never ventured into the heart of our fair town. They must have stayed on the bypass. This had to be so, because anyone taking the time to meander down our main street could not possibly arrive at so spurious a conclusion. Why, in just five minutes, a traveler can see thirteen motels, eleven convenience stores, and sixteen assorted fast-food outlets. While taking this tour one would be advised to listen to the soft renderings of one of our country and western radio stations. A really lucky first-time visitor might experience the deep philosophical growth associated with the popular tune "Your Wife's Been Running Around on Us Again." And they say there is no culture here.

Fuchs had a copy of the letter in front of him. He was shaking his head. "Fowler, this is inexcusable. It's insulting and shows a serious lack of teamwork. Personally, I think your letter is more derogatory than the damned article," he said, his voice rising slightly. "Will you write another, more appropriate, letter?" he asked.

"If you want my name on it, you've the only version I'll stand behind," I said, getting up.

Fuchs's smile told me he was pleased with my reaction. That bothered me a little. I hate to be predictable, and I didn't like pleasing the son of a bitch under any circumstances.

"Well, Fowler, you leave me no choice but to report this episode to President Brightal. Of course, I'll have to attach my personal evaluation of your handling of the entire matter," he said smugly.

37

The thought of my ass in a ringer with Brightal was more than the two of them could stand. Even Ed Andy was beginning to lighten up. He flashed that smile that had been responsible for selling a thousand GMC pickups.

"Boyd, you do whatever you feel up to doing," I said as I moved in the direction of the door. "Now boys, you will let me know if I can be of any further help?" I asked, and left without waiting for a reply.

On the way to my car I thought about the advisability of my course of action in this matter. I probably had succeeded in creating trouble further down the road. Brightal was a pretty good president, but he hated confrontation with a passion. If I'd given him some room, he'd have avoided conflict. Fuchs was sure to press this for all it was worth. What the hell, maybe this was one confrontation whose time had come. Fuchs was a liability. Maybe a good shoot-out would show Brightal what an asshole his old friend really was. In point of fact, Brightal had outgrown Fuchs and didn't yet realize it.

I had just enough time to go home and clean up. I wanted to be on time for my dinner with Case. I wanted to get the meeting over with as quickly as possible. A man ought to have clear focus on his priorities. I did.

∇

6

A Confused Case

T OMMY'S PLACE IS ACTUALLY named the Unicorn Pub. It's
my favorite haunt in town. A lot of that has to do with its
owner, Tommy Noonan. He's good people. We've been
friends since he opened the place about six years ago. He had
worked in taverns and bars throughout the state for years.
All the while, he had his sights set on owning his own pub
in a small college town. The Unicorn was the realization of
his lifelong dream. Not many people I know ever realize the
fullness of their dreams. It's nice when someone does. Maybe
it's my fondness for being a part of that that has made me
his best customer.

Tommy is a short, thick-necked little Irishman with arms
like ham hocks and a winning smile. Over the years we've
shared a few drinks and swapped a few tales. I like him for
a number of reasons, not the least of which is that he is a
bottom-line type of guy. No matter what the problem, when
the smoke clears and the shit settles, he'll be there with
you. He's an impulsive poker player and a pushover for
fair-haired colleens with bedroom eyes. Now that I think
about it, I guess he's not the only guy I know with those
weaknesses.

His pub is as close to Ireland as a person can get without
actually setting foot on the Emerald Isle. The decor is au-
thentic down to the dart boards and table accessories. The
bulk of his clientele consists of college faculty and graduate
students. Tommy serves a good drink and a good meal.

Case was already here. He was sitting in the booth we
usually occupied. Clearly, he was well into the evening. He
was nursing a Corona when I took the other bench. There

were three empties on the table. He was reading from a folder. He looked up and closed the report.

"Old buddy, you'll be glad to know that I've decided to allow the city of Nacogdoches to buy your supper," he said with a hint of beer-affected enunciation.

"Well hell, I'll not look a gift horse in the mouth. However, I think I will look at the menu for a change. Maybe Tommy has added something real expensive. I'm feeling exotic all of a sudden," I said.

"Oh shit, I wish I'd known," Case said with thin sincerity. "I already ordered for both of us. Just to save time and keep your mind clear while you look over these reports. I got me a couple of setters; I ordered you a chili dog and a diet soda."

"If there's one thing I admire in a public servant, it's a sense of fiscal responsibility. You cheap son of a bitch, what have you got for me to look at?" I asked.

The reports offered nothing new. Everything was about as I'd figured it would be. As I closed the last folder, the evening meal, such as it was, arrived. Case was dining light. The waitress placed two frosty mugs of green liquid in front of him. Tommy called these odd-looking concoctions Irish setters. They were the house specialty, a mix of Irish ale, two kinds of beer, and a mystery Irish whiskey. Tommy added food coloring for the green color. He felt it lent an Irish air to the offering. I'm told by my drinking friends, who are many, that this little dandy will pucker up all the orifices on your body. Case can drink a little beer. However, I thought the rate at which he was consuming Coronas and setters might stretch his range a mite. My chili dog, smothered in onions, was up to its usual high standard. I was glad that Case had ordered my Coke. I might've been tempted to order wine, and I can never remember which wine goes best with chili dogs.

"That big smile and your atypical generosity with city revenues tells me that you're extra happy about something. Want to fill me in?" I asked.

"We got a break a couple of hours ago. The state boys arrested a fella over in Tyler. He was tryin' to break into a

40

woman's house. They found a sack from a strip puke joint over on old fifty-nine. We checked and they remember him being there last night before the Wilson woman was killed. He denied ever being in town last night. When they showed him the sack, he asked for his lawyer." Case leaned back, smiled, and took a long drink on the first of his dinner entrees. He looked pretty smug. If I hadn't been already eating my pay I might simply have allowed him his fantasy.

"You satisfied that this fellow did the evil deed, are you?" I asked with a full mouth.

"Let's say that I'm satisfied that he fits all the evidence pretty goddamn well. I've suspected from the beginnin' that it was someone passin' through. Just took advantage of a situation. . . . You know, Fowler, not every murder is committed by a master criminal," he said with a touch of gibe.

"Thanks for that bit of information," I said as I wiped my mouth. "Where's this guy from? Does he have a record? Does he smoke exotic cigarettes?" I asked.

Out came the notebook. "His name is Jack Piligrew. He's a two-time loser for bad checks and drug possession. He's from Dallas. I don't know about the goddamn cigarettes," he concluded with little enthusiasm for the last bit of information.

I had an onion skin sliver caught in my teeth. Every time I eat one of those things, I get a sliver between my gum and a back tooth. It drives me crazy. With extraordinary tongue control, I exorcised it quickly.

"Where'd he say he was going that night?" I asked.

"Said he had a friend in Ennis. Stopped here for a bite."

I gave him my "is-that-all-there-is" look. He nodded that it was. I sipped on my drink and thought about what he'd told me. Case can't stand silence.

"Fowler, get it said," he said irritably.

"The Wilson woman wasn't raped and killed by Jack Piligrew," I said with a sigh. "She was killed by one, maybe two, professional killers. They're probably from the East Coast, and they were hired specifically to eliminate the Wilson woman."

41

I carefully watched Case as I outlined my theory. He showed little reaction. He finished his first setter.

"Well shit . . . that was my second theory," he said with a grin. "After all, it ain't that unusual for professional hit men to come to Nacogdoches and kill our excess spinsters. And as for the rape, well, they had some time on their hands. Lord, you've developed an imagination in your twilight years."

"There was no rape, at least not in the customary sense. The woman was killed. Strangled from behind. She was then laid on the bed and her clothes torn off. She was then cosmetically penetrated. It was a business bop, nothing more. A red herring to throw you off."

Case no longer looked calm. The veins were protruding on the sides of his neck. His look suggested a man who had just zipped up his pecker.

"Cosmetically penetrated?" he said a little too loudly for the surroundings. "What in the shit does that mean? A fake fuck? What in God's name are you talking about?" he asked as he attacked his second setter.

I waited for him to finish his drink. He needed a little time to calm down.

"There are a lot of little things that add up to only one conclusion," I argued. He slouched in the seat and motioned for me to continue.

"The room was wrong . . . wasn't messed up enough. The bed was too neat. A woman who has her clothes ripped from her body and is then strangled puts up a fight. She kicks and screams. She gets bruised and marked. Things get broken. Think about the scene. No blood, no bruises of consequence, and no semen. Hell, Case, the poker room looks worse than that bedroom. No, the woman was surprised from the rear. The killer wrapped the bra around her neck and lifted her off the floor. She had no leverage to struggle or wind to scream. After she was dead, the rape was staged." I paused to allow Case an opening for comment.

"Fowler, how in the hell did he strangle her with a bra the way you describe unless he'd already torn off her clothes before he killed her?" he asked with a bemused look.

42

"That's a major-league question, Case. I think, though, that you'll find that the bra around her neck probably wasn't the one she was wearing during the commission of the crime," I said. He looked on the verge of a mental breakdown. "If you look on the dryer you'll find a bra with bent and broken clasps. I figure he was going through her things when she came home. Oh, she was going to die all right, but he was looking for something, too. I don't know what. Anyway, he finds a bra lying around or in a drawer. He waits for her and kills her with it. As he tears off her clothes, it occurs to him that the package will be tighter if he leads us to believe the bra around her neck is the one she was wearing. He can't afford to take the one she was wearing with him. Too risky. He improvises and deposits it in her dirty laundry."

"Is that all there is to this fairy tale, or is there something else?" he asked.

"The method of entry was pro all the way. It's not the type of job a drugged-up bad-check passer could do. Hell, most cops wouldn't have noticed the entry marks," I said without mentioning anyone specifically.

"You still convinced that our boy came in through that window? Hell, we don't know that the front door, or for that matter the back door, wasn't open. He could've locked 'em before leavin' just to confuse us. Those window scratches would've come from something else." He was almost pleading now.

"Then there's the spiderweb in the guest bedroom and the dust pattern in the master bedroom," I said. His whole body sagged. "Case, there was a small broken spiderweb in the corner of the guest bedroom window. That window had been opened recently. On the other hand, the dust on the screen and the sill in the master bedroom was undisturbed. I don't think that window had been open in some time."

Case motioned to the waitress and she promptly brought him a fresh Corona. He took a swig and motioned for another.

"Let me get this straight. We got dust on the window sill, broken spiderweb, and a bra with straight clasps. With all

43

this solid evidence together it adds up to professional hit men comin' to town to kill one of our old women. I did get it all, didn't I? I need to have it all in order for when I go to the FBI." His voice had a noticeable edge.

"The man, or men, who killed Maureen Wilson waited for her for some time. Enough time to smoke several expensive cigarettes. The duplex was staked out. It's my guess that the killer waited by the tree until she left for the card game. I suspect he had a wheel man cruising the area to pick him up after the hit. Come on, Case, the Jack Piligrews of this world don't smoke expensive, handmade cigarettes from the East Coast. They also don't hang around for what might have been hours waiting for a victim to come home. If he wanted to rob the place, he'd have broken in before she got home. If it was rape he had on his mind, why assault the beast when a beauty lived next door?" I asked rhetorically.

Case got up and went to the bar. He came back with a bottle of Mescal and a shot glass. He took two shots and cleared his throat. He pulled out his plug.

"How do we know that those butts have anythin' to do with this killin' at all?" he asked. His voice had lost its aggressiveness. He was discouraged and it showed.

"You're reaching, Case. There are too many loose ends. As I recall, that's why you had me come over last night. Nothing was taken. There was some money in her drawers and pawnable things in the house. No tire tracks and no one saw a vehicle parked near the area. I'll bet you my mother's virtue that you won't be able to match Piligrew's prints with any of those you lifted from the scene." I was giving him an opening to reassess.

"Assumin' for a minute that all this fiction was fact, what in the hell is the motive? Who in Nacogdoches would know how to hire killers from the East Coast?" he asked.

"There you've got me. I don't have a clue. I guess that's one for the Angelina School of Law Enforcement." The humor missed. "As to who in town would know how to hire professional killers, that's a good question."

Beth came in and took a booth a few down from us. Case

and I were done for the night. It would be pointless to continue. He was in no condition to be rational. As a matter of fact, he was well on his way to becoming knee-walking, commode-hugging drunk.

"I think we've beat this horse to death," I said. "Why don't you go on home and think on it some. Tomorrow, when you feel human again, we'll kick it around some more."

I left him sitting there half mired in thought and half mired in stupor. I spied Tommy at the bar. I quietly motioned to him. He would see to it that Case got home.

7

Night as It Should Be

BETH WAS WEARING A light blue blouse and skin-tight jeans. She was ordering when I approached the table.

"Hello, sailor . . . want to buy a lonely woman a drink?" she asked in her most flirtatious voice. And nobody has a better flirting voice than a good Southern girl.

"You bet. My momma didn't raise no dumb sailors," I said, taking the seat across from her. "Well, lady, I was beginning to wonder if we were ever going to get any time alone."

"That thought crossed my mind, too," she said. "I was beginning to have doubts about your interest level." The waitress brought Beth's wine and asked if we wanted menus. Neither of us was hungry.

"Lady, I was interested the first time I saw you. But at the time, you were a student of mine. I don't like to confuse relationships," I explained.

"I've heard that about you. Tell me, though, do you see a problem with relationships with former students?" she asked almost matter-of-factly.

"That depends on the former student," I offered.

"That's nice to know," she said.

"Didn't I hear somewhere that you had become seriously involved with someone a couple of semesters back?" I asked.

"I got engaged last semester," she said between sips of wine.

Being a trained investigator I immediately picked up on the past tense of engage. I decided that a transparent expression of condolence for a past-tense relationship was appropriate.

46

"No lasting scars, I hope," I said.

She continued to sip the wine and looked at me sort of curiously. She was measuring her next comment.

"No scars," she said.

I was getting an uneasy feeling in the pit of my stomach. Recent semantics were not at all consistent with my earlier festive mood.

"Fowler . . . I got married in June," she said with a strange little smile.

Confused was my first reaction. Disappointed was my second. Pissed off was my third. Luckily, composure is one of my few virtues. In my best composed, grown-up voice I responded. "Who's the lucky man?"

"His name is Anson Sheffield. He's a lawyer in Houston. Does it bother you that I'm married?"

"I'm not sure. I've a friend who claims that married women pose the least threat to a single man." She leaned forward and rested her elbows on the table. She then rested her chin on her folded hands.

"God, this is brazen, even for me. Look, Fowler, like I said, the main reason I'm in town is to see you. The only reason I mentioned the marriage was to establish some boundaries. And there was always the possibility that you might have some of those rules of yours concerning married women. And heaven knows I wouldn't want to compromise your ethics," she concluded with a grin.

In the dim light her eyes were soft and inviting. I had a lot of questions on my mind. At the moment, however, the answers didn't seem all that urgent.

"This is a conversation best pursued elsewhere," I said, signing the ticket. We decided to leave her car at Tommy's.

When we got to the house, she walked to the fireplace and sat on the hearth. I stopped at the bar.

"Would you like something to drink?" I asked.

"No . . . I don't want something to drink," she said as she rose and took off her blouse.

I leaned against the bar and watched her slide out of her jeans. As good as she looked in jeans, she looked even better

47

out of them. Beth's body was lean and firm. She shed her underwear slowly . . . effortlessly. Her clothes folded neatly on the hearth, she sat down and put her hands behind her head and leaned back.

"Fowler, you're way behind," she said.

"Oh, I'll catch up soon enough. Lady, some moments are meant to be savored without distraction," I said as I started to take off my shirt. She came over and stopped me. She began to stroke my chest. Her lips were warm and moist. Her tongue was making a wet path down my chest and stomach. Her fingers had already settled on points south. By the time her mouth arrived, she had the situation well in hand. A number of women have passed through my life. Some were more memorable than others. The best of the lot couldn't compare with Beth when it came to plain old getting down to it.

She looked up from her knees and I motioned toward the bedroom. She shook her head. She grabbed my hands and pulled me toward the floor. A couple of things were becoming increasingly clear to me. Beth had spent damned little time in convents, and I was about to take a couple of years off my life.

She lay on the floor and opened to me. As I entered her, every muscle of her body responded. I slipped my hand under her arched back and pulled her off the floor and to me. Her fingers dug into my back and she buried her face in my chest.

We both lay motionless for several minutes. She rolled onto her stomach and I followed the contours of her body with my hand. Her skin was smooth and my trip down the yellow brick road ended where all such roads lead. Sex was redefined for me over the next couple of hours. I discovered angles I hadn't thought of since geometry. If ever there was a woman anatomically constructed with sex in mind, this was she.

She rolled over onto her back and lay there quietly. She seemed to be entranced by the blades of the ceiling fan. The French doors were open and the full moon threw its light across her naked body. I watched small droplets of sweat

48

form tiny streams that wound their way down her breasts and onto her stomach. It was the type of moment I tend to remember. I couldn't seem to take my eyes off the glistening moisture on her body.

"Fowler," she said in a soft, subdued voice, her eyes never leaving the fan, "want to satisfy a couple of nagging curiosities that have been bugging me for some time?"

"If you initiate every future interview this way, you're going to be a real successful reporter," I said.

"I'll keep that in mind," she said evenly. "We're not talking national security here, Fowler. Just a few little itches that I haven't been able to scratch," she said in her most soothing voice.

"So this is about curiosity?"

"My, my, the male mind is suspicious. Do you see me as having some hidden agenda?" she asked as she stretched and wiped the moisture from her abdomen.

"You win," I said slowly, wishing I'd wiped the sweat from her body. "What's on your mind? I've never considered myself complicated enough to pose a mystery for anyone. But I wouldn't want to repeatedly make love to a confused woman."

I wondered if she knew that disclosure tended to escalate relationships. As long as we kept it essentially physical, it was a no-cost proposition. We could put on our clothes and go our separate ways. Such escape is tougher when passion is mixed with compassion.

"What are you doing teaching in Naco-nowhere?" she asked quickly as if worried that I might change my mind.

"Which is the operative word, teaching or Nacogdoches?" I asked.

"Both, and don't start out by bullshitting me. You know damn well what I'm asking. Why does a man get a master's in forensic technology, then invest fifteen years of his life in the FBI? Then take a doctorate in constitutional law, leave the law enforcement field, write a best-selling book, and end up amongst the pine trees of east Texas." Her voice showed mock impatience.

49

"Methinks I've been taken," I said with due caution.

"I told you that I have been curious about you for some time," she said. "Besides, good newspaperwomen always research well."

"I'll keep that in mind in the future," I assured her. "I hate to disappoint you, but my reasons for being here aren't steeped in mystery or drama. I was a cop for a lot of years because that's what I grew up wanting to be. Then one day I decided that I didn't want to be a cop anymore. The crime business wears hard on a person. I wanted something with less edge to it. I decided that I wanted to teach. Being as Nacogdoches is my hometown, when the job at SFA became available, I jumped at it. I like the pace and the people, although sometimes I think I like them more than they like me. What the hell, everyone's got to be somewhere."

"Try as I do, I still can't picture you as a cop." She rolled over onto her side, facing me. She rested her head on her hands. "What was there about being a cop that caught your eye?"

"This is some really uninteresting stuff you're curious about. You sure you want to hear it?" I asked.

"Do I look bored to you?" she asked in return.

"No. Bored is not how you look."

"Well then, as soon as you've stalled enough, how about getting on with it," she suggested.

"I was convinced that I would've caught Thomas Crown. In my youth there were Moriartys that needed to be brought to justice. I wasn't unethical enough for politics, good-looking enough for Hollywood, or dull enough for growing soybeans. It came down to the ministry, narcotics, or law enforcement," I said with as much sincerity as I could muster under the circumstances.

"So what happened . . . run out of Moriarty types?" she asked.

"No, there's a limitless supply of Moriartys. I just grew up and went to town and saw the elephant. It finally became clear to me that we never catch the Moriartys. Oh, we know who they are, we even know where they are. But the legal

50

system is incapable of catching them. On the other hand, some poor, illiterate bastard staggers into a Stop and Go with an air pistol and robs them of thirty bucks which he promptly invests in drugs he hopes will kill the pain of his reality. We do catch him. Then we lock him away in an institution that hardens him so that the next time he uses a real gun and this time we execute him. His realities never change, and we'd rather kill him than change them."

"That's a bleak picture you paint there," she said quietly.

"Oh, it gets worse. Every day some white-collar type steals seven figures from the old, the ignorant, or the infirm. He either lives happily ever after in South America or hires F. Lee Getmeoff and beats the rap entirely. He gets born again, gives a few thousand to charity, hosts his own golf tournament, and eventually runs for public office. When I decided that I wasn't making much of a difference, I abandoned ship."

"I'll be damned if there's not a cynic buried deep under that ever optimistic veneer," she said with a thin smile. "But with your credentials, you could have taught anywhere in the country. Why here?"

"Well, let's see. . . . I don't like traffic, freeway construction, pollution of all types, urban crime, a constant view of inner-city poverty, and crowds in general. I'm partial to country roads, small cafés, clean space, and simplicity. Where better to escape the former and find the latter? Besides, it's home."

"You should be set up for a tough one," she said with a wicked grin. "How did your parents come up with the name Fowler?"

"That under-your-breath snicker didn't escape me," I warned. "Actually, my first name is William, after my father's father. My mother insisted on Fowler for reasons she, to this day, refuses to discuss. The fact that no one on her side of the family has that name and the fact that I don't resemble anyone on either side of the family has long been a source of considerable concern for my father," I said with total sincerity.

She rolled her eyes and appeared skeptical of the answer.

51

"Willie, we're going to have major problems with this arrangement if your answers continue to smell of fiction," she scolded.

I mustered my best hurt look.

"You might want to reconsider that reaction. I will not be repeatedly taken advantage of by a woman who doesn't trust me. I'm not simply a sex object, you know. . . . I have some pride."

"How much pride?" she asked curtly.

"It's negotiable. But enough about me. How about a little reciprocation here? How about scratching a few itches for me? Tell me about you and Anson."

"Married young. Too young and for mostly the wrong reasons. When it fell apart, I met Anson. He was in the middle of a deteriorating relationship himself. We provided strength to each other for a long time. Early on, the passion was strong. Maybe the intensity was a substitute for insight. Looking back on it, I think we were both running so fervently from things that we never really considered where we were running to. Eventually, the relationship became a habit. There's not a lot of passion in a habit. We generated more heat tonight than Anson and I ever have." Her eyes never left mine.

I watched her face in the moonlight. There was a second, and not much more, when her eyes glistened with moisture and she seemed very vulnerable. Then, as if by command, her in-control smile reappeared.

"Don't get worried," she explained. "I'm not a cow-eyed young coed looking for a long-term relationship. I've got a realistic perspective on the evening."

"You said earlier that your primary reason for coming back to town was to see me. What other reasons were there?" I asked as I stroked her hair.

"I've finished all the course work on my master's. The thesis has been a bit of a problem. I just haven't been able to settle on a solid project. I had hoped to finalize a topic for the paper while I was here," she said without much confidence in her voice.

"Don't press," I advised.

"Easy for you to say," she said. "But enough on the mundane aspects of the present. Let's hear about the love life of Willie Fowler McFarland. It's only fair . . . I mean my love life is laid open in front of you. I think equal footing is called for here."

"At last count, I'd been in love three times. The first time was with a little girl in the fifth grade. Her name was Jackie Elliot. She had great big eyes and was the first girl in elementary school to develop breasts and wear tight skirts. I loved her for a long time . . . from a distance, of course. Later, I fell head-over-heels in love with a sixty-seven splitback Vet and later still with a four-hundred-pound, solid-oak poker table."

"Is that right? Well, the car is in the driveway and the table is sitting over there. That just leaves the girl. Whatever happened to her anyway?" she asked.

"As I understand it, the lady in question has long been married to a man undoubtedly not up to her standards. I hear she has three kids and lives somewhere around Texarkana," I concluded.

"So, the one real true love of your life got away?" she asked.

"Ain't that always the way of things," I replied.

"Well, I recall a number of nubile coeds looking at you with more than an 'I have a question, Dr. McFarland' look," she said. "It's hard to imagine that, given the traffic, you haven't been able to find any passable relationships." Her gaze was intense. I've always wondered why women seem so interested in a man's past love life. I've always felt that the less I knew, the better.

She moved closer to me and put her hand on my hip.

"There's such intense softness in your eyes. How many women have you seduced with those eyes, Fowler McFarland?" she asked, her voice getting very soft.

"Elizabeth Sue Bush, you should know by now that women can't be seduced. Only girls can be seduced, and damn few of them."

"You're a dangerous man, mister."

She slid over and gently rolled me onto my back. She rested her head on my lap and I stroked that chestnut hair while we lay there silent for several minutes. I was in no hurry to end the moment. It was one I wanted to hold on to for as long as possible. Eventually, I pulled a couple of pillows from the hearth. She was asleep as I placed her head on a pillow and covered her with my fireplace afghan. The last sounds I heard were those of the crickets, the faint hum of the fan, and the rhythm of her breathing.

8

Loose Ends

THE NEXT MORNING I awoke to find Beth up and gone. There was a note on the microwave that said she'd left me a couple of donuts and some milk. I pushed a sausage link through each of the donuts and nuked them in the microwave. It's a dish I call a "honeymoon breakfast."

The previous night's activities had taken something of a toll on me. For the first time in my life, I understood fully the expression "rode hard and put away wet." I took a slightly longer, more scenic route to the campus. I drove slowly to allow the morning air to clear my head a little. I got bold and turned on the radio. I didn't catch the name of the country and western song that was playing, but as always, the lyrics were memorable. My favorite line was "My wife's done run off with my best friend . . . and I miss him."

My student secretary, Kristin Santilli, was trying to figure out how to use the new computer as I passed through to my office. I wanted to know more about Beth's husband so I called Chris Lion. He had been in charge of the research staff of the *Houston Chronicle* for twenty-plus years. He's one of the best-informed people I know. More importantly, he knows where to lay his hands on information he doesn't possess.

"Chris, this is Fowler. How are you doing?" I asked.

"I'm doing well, thank you. Things continue to go on in your absence from the big city. Fowler, what do you need to find out?" he asked knowingly.

"Hell, Chris, what makes you think I have a motive other than simple salutations?" I asked in my most hurt voice.

"Fifty dollars says that this conversation will not end

without your asking me to dig up something," he countered.

"I'm deeply shocked that you think me so shallow as to disguise ulterior motives in a friendly call," I replied. "However, get me everything you've got on a local lawyer named Anson Sheffield."

"It'll cost you," he warned.

"Can I afford this service?" I asked.

"Next time you're in town we take in the Astros. Your treat, of course. On the way we'll need to stop at Casa Yo' Momma's for ribs and enchiladas. Your treat, of course," he concluded.

"Works for me," I said.

"How soon do you need the stuff?" he asked.

"As soon as possible."

"Thanks for the usual slack," he quipped. "I'll get back to you sometime today."

I was pondering the type of guy Beth would marry, when the phone brought me back to reality. It was Billy Bob Butterman reminding me that there was a Judicial Committee meeting during the noon hour. Several years back, the administration was advised by an expensive management firm to establish a lot of committees composed of faculty and administrators. These committees were to oversee a wide range of school policies and activities. They had names like Staff and Development, Affirmative Action, and Judicial. The idea behind their creation was to give the faculty the illusion that they had substantial input into the making of school policy. Actually, the higher administration ignored committee decisions that weren't consistent with their own. The committees did offer the administration a scapegoat on decisions where controversy was involved. In those cases the committee would be guided to the policy desired by the administration, then the powers that be would plead to the public that their hands were tied by a committee decision.

I'm a member of the Judicial Committee. Its purpose is to serve as an appeals board for students who have been issued citations by the campus security officers. If a student feels that a citation is unfair, he comes before the committee

56

and gets a hearing. In the four years I've been on the committee, it has heard possibly a hundred cases. During that time, I've voted with the majority three times. It would be fair to say that I'm not in the mainstream.

This meeting was a repeat of past efforts. Billy Bob Butterman, the chairman of the committee, pulled me to one side and told me that I just didn't seem capable of seeing the big picture. As I walked back to my office, I tried to grasp what that was. I eventually came to the conclusion that it was probably my destiny to see the world through a small lens.

There was a message from Kristin when I got back, saying that Chief Bayhill wanted to have dinner at the Unicorn at 6:00 P.M.

Beth was waiting for me.

"As I recall the waning moments of consciousness last night, it was my turn to ask you a question," I said.

"Ah . . . so it was," she said.

"You're off the hook for the moment, but I won't forget it," I said firmly.

"Well all right, but I claim my right of selective proxemic disclosure," she threw out with a grin.

I wasn't used to women with larger vocabularies than my own. I refused to humble myself and ask for clarification. There is pride in ignorance.

"I don't recall any disclaimers or stipulations in the original agreement," I protested.

"Fine print . . . it's a tough world out there. If you want to pry information from me you'll have to place me in the proper environment. I've discovered that I lose my informational inhibitions at your apartment in the throes of physical exhaustion. I'm afraid that if you want another answer from me, you'll just have to invite me back over."

"This smacks of extortion. You know there are limits to how much I will prostitute my body simply to satisfy my curiosity," I warned.

"Is that right? What's the limit?"

"I'll not be tricked that easily," I said. "It's your turn to answer the questions."

She walked over and looked out the window. She was working up to something. I decided to give her room to maneuver. She turned around and clasped her hands and popped her fingers. She took a "what the hell" breath and came back over and sat down. She was ready.

"Fowler . . . I want you to help me investigate the Maureen Wilson murder as the basis for my master's thesis," she said with aggressive speed, but tentative inflection. "You know , it would require me to spend a lot of time in the area. Otherwise, I guess I'll just mosey on back to Houston for the remainder of the year."

The possibility of Beth going back to Houston just then wasn't pleasant.

"What direction do you want to take in the paper?" I asked. I worked at sounding noncommittal.

"I was thinking about a chronology of a murder investigation in a small town. Where else could I learn as much about real, hands-on investigation than you?" she asked, knowing she'd built a good case.

"It'll have to be okay with Case Bayhill. He's a good friend as well as the chief of police. I don't want to get in his way. And you'll have to get the approval of your committee. I'm having dinner with Case again tonight. I'll ask him up front."

"Do you think he'll balk at the idea?" she asked.

"I'm not real sure. There's an election coming up and he's facing his first real challenge in several years. This murder comes at a bad time," I said.

"I'll bet the farm that you'll be able to convince him," she said.

"All of this may be a little premature, however, unless your advisers okay the plan. Who's your primary adviser?" I asked.

"Dr. Fox is the appointed adviser and Dr. Creel has agreed to assist. Haven't approached a third faculty member yet."

"Well, both of them are out of town right now. Creel is at a convention in Seattle and Fox is in Houston having his hemorrhoids snipped. Given the size of Fox, I expect those are some monster 'rhoids. The longer it takes you to get their permission, the colder the trail gets," I cautioned.

"I'll have their permission not later than tomorrow night," she said matter-of-factly. "I assume that I can inform Dr. Fox that I've located my third adviser?"

"I've come this far . . . what the hell," I replied.

I love to see confidence and enthusiasm in combination. It's the best thing about college students. I didn't see any idle puffing in Beth and was pretty sure that Fox and Creel were in the bag.

"You've got a class," she said as she looked at her watch. "I've got work to do." She turned and headed for the door.

"Are we going to continue twenty questions tonight?" she asked without turning around. Without seeing her, I knew she would be sporting her wickedest smile.

"I'll be home sometime past nine. I'll leave the door open," I answered.

"I thought I could count on your curiosity above all other motives," she whispered as the door closed.

The ringing of the phone broke my train of thought.

"I believe you were interested in a profile on a Mr. Anson Argon Sheffield," the voice said. I quietly cringed. Someone named their human offspring Argon. It sounded like a gasoline additive.

"He's thirty-six years old. Born in Houston to wealthy parents. His daddy was in real estate when that was a good thing to be in. Attended private schools and was an excellent student. Graduated magna cum laude from Cornell. Top ten percent of his law class at Emory. Took a position with Bitner, Branton and Bradshaw in Houston. Must have impressed the big boys . . . two years ago he was made the youngest partner in the firm's history."

"Is the son of a bitch a Nobel candidate?" I asked weakly.

"No mention of it here," he said dryly.

"What a relief," I snapped. "What does the guy look like?" I asked.

"He's a big, good-looking guy. I've a picture of him playing in a charity tennis tournament. Want me to send it along?" he asked.

"Why not?" I responded.

59

"His driver's license says he's six feet two inches tall and weighs one hundred and seventy-five pounds. He looks like something created for California. You know—blond, blue, and brown. He's a marathon runner, a scratch golfer, and a championship club tennis player. You need any more of this sort of stuff?" he asked.

"No, I think I've got a grip on his athletic shortcomings," I mumbled.

"You interested in his family situation?" he asked.

"What the hell, go for it," I said.

"He's been married twice. His first wife was his childhood sweetheart. Good family and a lot of money. You know the type. River Oaks and all that. They were divorced a couple of years ago. Don't have any details on that. They weren't the society page type. He remarried a few months back. The latest Mrs. Sheffield is something of a departure from the first. She's from north Houston. Middle-class stock. A working girl who went to public schools. I don't have a picture of her, but I doubt that you need one. I see here that she is a college student at SFA. . . . Gee, what a coincidence," he chirped.

"Spare me, will you? Don't let your mind get subterranean on me. You got anything on his finances?"

"I don't have anything. I can probably get it for you, but it'd be a waste of time. The man comes from old money and has to be in high six figures with the law firm."

"Is there anything negative about the guy?" I asked with little hope of relief.

"I'm happy to say that this guy is squeaky clean. If I had to guess, I'd guess he bleeds milk and farts perfume. There is one thing. It might just be the picture, but the guy has skinny legs." He chuckled, knowing I wasn't having fun.

I went to class trying to understand why Beth was here.

$\bigtriangledown$

9

Hob and Case

THURSDAY EVENINGS ARE GENERALLY a little slow at the Unicorn. Tommy tends bar and lets one girl handle the table traffic. Business picks up about eight o'clock when the night classes begin to release. The place was nearly deserted when I entered. The only other patron was Hob Bigby. He was holding up one end of the bar and talking to Tommy.

Hob is long on personality and is usually on an up. He's a diminutive gnome on the wrong end of fifty. I like Hob. He's interesting. I've decided that his life focus is centered around two characteristics. He's cheap, and he's the least discriminate womanizer I've ever seen. If an organism possesses any trace of estrogen, has a discernible pulse, and is slow enough of foot, Hob will try to mount it.

"Had any quiff lately?" I asked.

"Hell no. The price of cheese being what it is," he answered.

I got a Coke and took a seat. Hob was nursing a Bloody Mary. Tommy wasn't drinking. He was soaking up Hob's wisdom.

"I tell you, men, they're all the enemy. They bitch about being abused and discriminated against. Like hell. They control two-thirds of the money and all of the quiff," he growled.

Hob was well known for his theories about the innate adversarial relationship between men and women. He had expounded on the subject many times before.

"Is this a reaction to any particular woman or is it a broad indictment of women in general?" I asked with caution. When Hob combined alcohol and anxiety he was very philosophical.

"Only one of the vipers has me in her sights at the moment, but they're all the same. It's an estrogen conspiracy. It's enough to make a man think about turnin' gay," he said sadly.

It's comforting to know that even an old womanizer like Hob can get confused. I didn't feel alone in my stupidity. As to why finding another stupid person should make one feel better, I can't say.

I felt a hand on my shoulder. It was Case.

"Boys . . . Everythin' all right this evenin'?" he said as he took a seat next to me.

"We were just discussing the liabilities of female companionship," Hob explained.

"I'm real sorry I missed that," Case said as he ordered a Corona.

"What's the latest on Nacogdoches's night killer?" Hob asked.

"We got a few leads and a suspect in custody," Case said as he poured his beer into an iced mug. I expected it was an answer he'd given to scores of newspeople the last few hours. He had it down pat.

Hob nodded his approval. "It's not that I'm worried for myself, you understand. The son of a bitch seems to prefer spinsters. But anyone crazy enough to rape the Wilson woman might be crazy enough to find me attractive. I'll sleep a lot better knowing you're on the job," he said as he headed for the men's room.

Case looked at me and smiled a little. "Old Hob's got a snootful tonight. What's the occasion?" he asked.

"His latest concubine must be pressing him for commitment," I answered.

"Let's talk a bit," Case said as he headed for a table.

Case took off his hat and wiped his brow. His uniform was soaked through. His face was a little drawn. "It's a mother out there tonight," he said.

"Yeah . . . it's likely to be a hot, wet night," I agreed.

Case nursed his beer a little and looked more at the table than at me. I let him get it all straight in his mind.

"I'm thinkin' 'bout goin' with Piligrew on the Wilson killin'. There are a few loose ends. But we're workin' on 'em. We'll work 'em out eventually," he said, finishing his beer with a long, pleasing drink.

He looked at me for comment. I didn't offer any.

The upcoming election was probably weighing heavily on his mind. Until this year, he'd always run unopposed. Buck Meadows had changed all that. He was a well-to-do local rancher who was bored with ranching and eager to play politics. He looked around and decided that the chief of police job was the most accessible. Normally it wouldn't be, but Case's inability to solve the Congrady killing earlier in the year had given Meadows some political leverage in the town.

Case shouldn't have been held accountable for the killer of Beayne Congrady never being caught. It was an unsolvable case. Eccentric old woman found dead in her shack in the woods. No clues, no motive, and no hope of a solution.

"You're treading on thin ice if you try to fit Piligrew for this killing. It just might explode in your face," I said.

Case was thumping his fingers on the table and playing with the salt and pepper shakers.

"Why not avoid formally arresting him for the Wilson killing for a few days. Book him on something else. Just keep him under wraps for a few days. Stick to your patented answer and don't be prodded into doing or saying anything rash. Give me a couple of days and I might be able to find out something that'll help."

"You know somethin'?" he asked.

"No. But I agree with something you said earlier. The key is finding the motive. I'd like a couple of days to dig around and see if I can uncover a reason for her to be murdered," I said.

Case sat back and looked at me thoughtfully. "Old buddy, I hope I don't live to regret this. . . . A couple of days, huh?" he asked.

"Give me as much as you can. Hell, if I wash out, you can always blow some smoke with Piligrew," I said.

Case dropped a couple of bills on the table. He finished

the last of his beer. I thought he was going to say something, but I guess he thought better of it. He got up and put his hat on.

"One last thing," I said. "I'm going to need some help on this. I think I'll use one of my graduate students to do some of the legwork. So don't get spooked if you hear her digging around. Her name is Beth Sheffield."

"Jesus H. Christ, what have I got myself into? My ass is in the hands of a schoolteacher and a piss-ant student." He shook his head in disbelief and walked out.

The place was filling up. I tried to size up the situation as it now looked. I needed to solve the murder. I needed to do it in such a way as to make Case look good. I needed to milk a master's thesis out of the investigation. While doing these things, I needed to try and make sense of a relationship that had me thoroughly confused. Hell, I guess looked at like that it was pretty simple.

Del Shannon was wailing about his runaway when I parked the car. I scrounged up a couple of pieces of old pizza. I was about to put them into the microwave when I decided that they looked a little anemic. I turned it into a more delectable offering by adding breakfast sausage, onions, bologna strips, and Colby cheese. I nuked the whole mess and settled down for a unique culinary experience. I switched on the answering machine. Only one message. My dad wanted me to come to Splendora for a family barbecue on Saturday.

I'd just finished listening when the door literally flew open and Beth almost danced in. The entrance combined with an unbridled smile told me that, as expected, she had gotten the permission of Creel and Fox.

"Okay, lady, tell me how you did it so quickly," I said.

"Creel was easy. I ran him down by phone. Fox was a little more difficult. I drove to Houston and caught up with him in recovery. He was lying on his stomach under the influence of something wonderful. I came armed with flowers and my best get-well smile." She paused and flashed the smile for me. I know it made me feel better immediately. "He was very supportive of the plan. They both were. Now, how about your end of the deal?" she asked. I'm not sure she had breathed during the entire monologue. She grimaced at the sight of my dinner and looked a little ill.

"Like you, I went to Case with my best get-well smile and he was overwhelmed. He agreed to let us get involved in the investigation." I wasn't finished, but I didn't get the chance. She leaped from the barstool onto my lap without her feet ever touching the floor.

"Hold on, there's a little more to this conversation with Case. We're committed to conducting this investigation with some consideration to the upcoming election," I said.

"What does that mean?" she asked.

"It means that I don't want to cost my best friend his job by embarrassing him. If we discover anything of importance, I want to funnel it to him. We're not in this to scoop his office."

She went to the refrigerator and got a beer. "What if we find out that his people are way out in left field. From what you've told me, they don't exactly agree with your view of the killing."

"Case will ultimately do the right thing. If we find that he's on the wrong track, I want him to have the opportunity to right himself before the papers get the scent," I explained.

"Deal," she said.

Beth's look told me she was through talking. The pizza was gone. It seemed that we were left with only one thing to do. At risk of life and limb, she moved forward and kissed me long and hard. Considering my dinner, I figured my breath would knock a buzzard off a shitwagon. It didn't slow her down. It was either true love or she actually liked the taste of the pizza.

This time we made our way into the bedroom. The moment we were close all the problems of the day seemed to disappear. I've been attracted to a number of women in my life, but none like this. This was noncognitive and addictive. That part of it bothered me. Not enough, however, for me to stop or think it through before going on. When I was fourteen my father cautioned me about letting the little head do the thinking for the big head. Maybe this was the classic case of a male mid-life crisis. On the other hand, maybe not every aspect of some relationships can be explained rationally. Maybe some feelings don't make sense. In the face of confusion, I did what I always do. I yielded to the hedonistic instincts in me and went with the flow.

The next two hours were largely unencumbered by conversation. Eventually I ended up lying on my back with Beth lying on top of me. Her head was on my chest.

"How'd you and Case Bayhill become such good friends?" she asked quietly.

"Goes back a long time. We've been friends for a lot of years. I grew up in a middle-class family here in Nacogdoches. I didn't exactly blend in with the Nacogdoches way of looking at things. I didn't like country and western anything. I was the smartest kid in school and a tad too liberal. I wasn't your basic good old boy."

"That makes you two a strange pair," she injected.

"There's some truth in that. Case was the toughest kid in school. He was one of five kids raised on a farm outside of town. His folks were poor. We're talking Nacogdoches poor here. I mean they didn't have a pot to piss in. His daddy, Raff, was a bitter man. He drank too much and every so often he took his frustrations out on the kids. Case was the oldest, and early on, he took it upon himself to spare his brothers and sisters by taking the brunt of his daddy's ire. I remember seeing him come to school with all sorts of temporary disfigurement. Mr. Bayhill never held a job for any period of time. His wife worked, but she died when Case was eleven or so. By the time he was fifteen, Case was the breadwinner in the family. He worked a couple of jobs. One of them was at the grocery store in my neighborhood. That's where we became friends. I worked there as well. Every other Friday old man Fetterman would lock Case and me in the store overnight to restock the shelves."

"Is Case his Christian name?" she asked.

"His real name is Wensel Orley Bayhill. He was given the name Case by our old football coach, Mr. Erickson. It was

66

his view that he transformed boys into men. He was uniformly disliked by all those he had forced into his version of manhood. One night someone locked up a couple of ducks in his new Camaro. It had a white, rolled-and-tucked interior. Come the next morning, the Chevy had depreciated significantly."

"God, that's an awful picture," she said through a frown.

"Ain't it though. Anyway, Erickson had it in his head that it was one of the football team who'd done the deed. He made us all strip naked and line up around the swimming pool. He tried to bully us into telling him who the culprits were. Finally, he singled out Case to tell him the name of the guilty parties. Case told him that he didn't know who'd done it. The son of a bitch started to give Case swats with a board. When you're buck-ass naked, the damn thing takes a toll. After a dozen or so licks, he stopped and asked Case again. Case gave him the same answer. He didn't protest the abuse, he didn't cry, and he didn't tell. Erickson would hit him three or four times and then stop and ask him the same question every time. Case gave him the same answer each time. It ceased being a quest for the guilty and became a clash of wills."

"How many times did the son of a bitch hit him?" she asked.

"Hell, I don't recall, but eventually Erickson got so arm-weary he couldn't swing the board. I can still see Case standing there with blood dripping down his legs. He just stood there. Pain simply meant nothing to him. Erickson called him a hard case and the 'case' part of the name stuck."

"That's a tough way to earn a nickname," she offered.

"It proved to be prophetic later. There were a number of members of that team who didn't like me much. The leader of that group was Ed Andy Andrews. He was an offensive tackle on a line that was dubbed by the local sports page as 'the five blocks of granite,' after the famous Notre Dame line. At the time, I was the editor of the high school paper. I wrote a story suggesting that the nickname related more to their IQ than it did to their football prowess."

67

"Fowler, how bright do you figure it is to piss off a Neanderthal the size of a truck?" she asked, smiling.

"Being dumb is a part of being a teenager. One night over at Beefy's, Ed Andy showed up a little drunk. He saw my car and decided to enjoy himself at my expense. Of course, a crowd gathered and he tried to induce me to fight him. I stood about six feet tall and weighed a hundred and sixty. I was giving away six inches and eighty pounds. He succeeded in provoking me into a position where fighting seemed my only viable option. My head said stupid, but my pride said stand up to him. He milked it for all it was worth. I decided that my only chance lay in getting in the first blow. I gave him my best right cross. It caught the asshole flush in the face. A slight cut opened below his left eye. Blood began to trickle down his cheek. His first punch caught me on the side of the head. It was a glancing blow. He followed the first with a second that found the middle of my forehead. I was stunned to the point of losing focus. Things got fuzzy for a few seconds. The next thing I heard was Case's voice. He must've showed up during the fight. He told Ed Andy to leave it alone, that I'd had enough. Ed was having too much fun and feeling the alcohol too strongly to pay any attention, even to Case. Ed took a step toward me, and Case stepped in between us. Case's first punch broke Ed Andy's nose. It split open like a ripe zucchini. His second shot landed above Ed Andy's right eye. The force of the blow combined with his class ring to tear off Ed Andy's right eyebrow. It splattered on the windshield of my car. I leaned against the fender and watched it ooze down to the wipers."

"Well, baby, you don't look much the worse for the wear," she said brushing the hair from my forehead.

"I went off to Texas and Case went to Angelina Community College. Ed Andy became mayor and Case the chief of police."

"Is this investigation the payback?" she asked.

"I like to see it as a favor both for an old friend and for a new friend," I responded. She rolled off me and assumed her sleeping position next to me. I put my arms around her and prepared to slip off.

"Fowler," she whispered. "I'd sleep a lot better if you'd tell me one more thing."

"Lady, you're the most curious person I've ever molested."

"Where'd you get the ducks?" she asked evenly.

"Kiss my ass. That's not a question. It's an accusation. I won't honor it with an answer," I said firmly. "Now go to sleep." My last conscious thought was that Anson Argon Sheffield had better be a hell of a man.

▽

10

The Beginning Scent

I AWOKE TO FIND Beth still asleep. I arose very quietly so as not to wake her. I got almost to the kitchen when I heard a voice from behind me. "What's for breakfast?" she asked sleepily.

"So you were faking it, huh," I said. "As for breakfast, I'm sure we'll be able to find something biodegradable in there." I pointed to the refrigerator.

She sauntered into the kitchen and peered into the refrigerator. She was clad only in a pair of socks. With her back to me, standing with the refrigerator door open, she asked in her most sincere voice, "See anything here you want?"

This was one of those times in a man's life when he has to take control. To yield to this obvious female chauvinist ploy would start our investigation off on the wrong foot. I held my breath and bit my tongue. "How about some juice," I said and headed for the bathroom.

When I got back to the kitchen, Beth was wearing one of my Stephen F. Austin T-shirts.

"How long can you stay in Nacogdoches?" I asked.

"As long as it takes," she said firmly. "Where do we stand?"

"Professional killers are expensive and you don't look for 'em in the yellow pages. Find out why she was killed and the 'who' will probably be clear," I said.

"What about inheritance?" she asked while buttering a piece of toast. "Maybe an obscure relative died and left her some money and one of the other heirs is greedy."

"Avarice is always a good motive. Don't forget a scorned lover, a person from her past who has a hate for her, perhaps a revenge killing related to someone close to her. It usually has to do with money, love, or hate," I suggested.

"We need to dig into her life. I'll pry into her deep background. I know a few shortcuts. You look into the last five years or so. I'll be at Tommy's at three. If we don't connect then, I'll see you here at six," I said.

"I'll start with the high school where she taught," Beth said as she started for the bathroom.

I had access to several newspaper morgues from my bureau days. I was dressed and on my way out when the bathroom door opened and Beth stuck her head out.

"We got any chance of pulling this thing off?" she asked with water streaming down her face.

"There are no perfect murders where motives and specific victims are involved. It's just a matter of perseverance, research, and maybe a little luck," I offered.

She started to close the door and resume her shower. I stopped her by putting my hand on the door.

"Might save a lot of time if you stayed here for the next few days," I suggested.

She looked at me with those big eyes, made bigger still by the wet puppy effect. She thought for a second. "I better not. Even Anson has his limits. Not to mention me," she said, closing the door.

On the way to the office I stopped by the police station and talked to Case. I told him that Beth would probably be in to see him today. I got the name and number of the woman who'd reported the crime. Her name was Helen Burris. I called her from his office, and she agreed to meet me at her house in fifteen minutes. She seemed excited about being interviewed by a journalist. All right, it was a stretch.

The Burris house was located in the oldest part of town. It was, in fact, on one of the two original streets in Nacogdoches. It was a large, white frame house sitting on concrete blocks. It had one of those large porches that appear to surround the entire ground floor of the house. Like all the yards on the street, hers was immaculately landscaped. I parked under a huge crepe myrtle next to a bed of giant red cannas. I noticed two women on the porch. The heat was oppressive;

they were seated around a lawn table with a large pitcher of lemonade. The were both wearing bright flowered cotton sundresses complete with matching hats. I suspected that those frocks were part of the K mart Scarlett O'Hara garden collection.

I stopped at the base of the steps and introduced myself.

"Hello, ladies, I'm Fowler McFarland." I could feel the sweat starting to form under my clothes.

The woman with the bright yellow flowers on her dress offered her hand. I gladly moved up the steps and into the shade of the porch. The other woman was introduced as Mrs. Carter, a neighbor. She would forever serve as a witness to the day that Helen Burris was interviewed about the murder of her friend. I took out a tape recorder and placed it next to the lemonade. They exchanged the looks of women who knew about these sort of things.

"I hope you ladies don't mind if I tape our conversation?" I asked. "It's so much more accurate than relying on one's memory."

Mrs. Burris offered me some lemonade. I hate the stuff, but for diplomatic purposes, I accepted. I'm sure that cat piss must approximate the flavor.

"How long had you known Miss Wilson?" I asked.

"My goodness, I guess we were friends for over twenty years," she said, looking at Mrs. Carter for confirmation. "Maureen moved to town in 1966."

"Where did she move from?"

"She was from Tyler. She lived there all her life until she came here," she said sadly.

"Did Miss Wilson ever discuss why she moved here?" Again, the two women exchanged looks that only intensely knowledgeable old biddies can flash. "Her parents were killed in a fire. You understand. She came here to start over," she replied.

I noticed my lemonade glass. It was one of those you get free with the purchase of some minimum amount at the grocery store. This must be the Disney series. Mine had Goofy on it. I thought that appropriate.

"Did Miss Wilson have any steady male friends?" I asked

72

as delicately as I could. It was clear that the question was bothersome to the ladies. "I know how delicate this subject is, but I'm sure that you're aware how often violent crimes such as this one are caused by love gone sour," I added.

Mrs. Carter nodded affirmatively and Mrs. Burris decided it was all right. "Maureen was a fine, Christian woman. She wasn't one to flutter about. She did have one male friend. His name is Jubal Lee Baker. He's a taxidermist with a shop in his garage. His place is over off of Delmar Street. It was mostly going to church together and an occasional movie. We spoke about him a couple of times. She allowed as she was fond of him."

"As far as you know, Mr. Baker was the only man in her life," I said.

"I think so. After my Jim died, we talked about men a little. She enjoyed their company occasionally, but had no need of it. She was very set in her ways," she said.

I finished off the lemonade, put Goofy on the table, and thanked Mrs. Burris with a smile.

"Did she have any hobbies or favorite activities?" I asked. As I was asking the question I noticed a very large cockroach crawling down a leaf on the banana tree that overlapped the porch railing. The bastard was big enough to carry off the lemonade pitcher. I remembered my mother telling me that roaches hated banana trees and that the best way to cut down on the roach population in your house was to plant a lot of banana trees around the place. Another bubble from my youth burst before my eyes.

Without any unusual effort and without interrupting the flow of her conversation at all, Mrs. Burris took off a shoe and smashed the prehistoric holdover into a pulp which reminded me of those ice cream bars that have a chocolate covering around a vanilla center.

"Well, she liked to play cards. We played hearts and occasionally a little bridge. She liked to bowl and, of course, she was very active in the church. She worked very hard at her school. She liked to stay busy," she said as she put her shoe back on.

I got up and wandered over to the back section of the porch. From here the backyard was visible.

"Mighty healthy tomatoes," I said.

"My Jim and I always kept the best garden on the street. It was bigger then. Now that he's gone, a few beans, some squash, and those tomatoes are all I can handle," she said, obviously pleased that I had noticed her garden.

"Did Miss Wilson have any enemies that you know of?" I asked.

"Lord no," she said without hesitation. "She wasn't always the easiest person in the world to get along with, but I don't know of anyone who really disliked her."

Mrs. Carter gave her a look as if to say that she disagreed with the last answer.

"Well, I guess there was one person who didn't get along with Maureen," she said, looking at Mrs. Carter. "She and Myra, that's Myra Colleridge, once had words about the use of the church gym. They were both on the recreation committee of the Baptist church. One summer the gym at the Catholic church burned down. They asked if their basketball team could use the Baptist gym until theirs was rebuilt. Maureen was very firm in her belief that the Baptist gym ought to be reserved for Christians and she considered Catholics to be pagans. Myra's sister married a Catholic, and Myra objected to Maureen's calling them pagans. They got into a heated and unladylike exchange outside of church one Sunday. They made quite a spectacle, I must say. Myra never forgave Maureen for that afternoon's remarks. But what in the world could this have to do with her death? Wasn't she killed by a sex fiend?" she asked.

"Probably nothing, but it's one of those standard questions," I responded. "Did she have any close relatives living anywhere in the general area?" I asked quickly.

"There is one, I believe. Yes, there is an aunt she used to talk to on the phone every month. I recall Maureen driving over to see her a time or two. She lives in Tyler. Let me see. Her name is Osceola Wilson. She's got to be near on to eighty by now," she said.

"Had Miss Wilson always been a teacher?" I asked.

"As long as I've known her. She taught court reporting over at the junior college for a number of years before she came to the high school. She dearly loved to teach, you know," she said.

I turned off the recorder. I thanked the ladies for their help and told them I'd get back to them if any more questions came to mind. Mrs. Carter couldn't let me leave without asking when the interview would be in the papers. I told them I wasn't sure but I'd see they both got copies.

As I cranked up the car and turned on the air conditioner, I watched as both women made for the indoors. Judging from their speed, I suspected that every old woman in town would know about the interview by dinner. I decided to try a flyer. I stopped by a small restaurant and used the pay phone. Information listed one Osceola Wilson in Tyler. The voice that answered the phone didn't sound like an eighty-year-old woman's. It was clear and aggressive. She wasn't nearly as thrilled as the previous ladies were about being interviewed. It wasn't until I told her that there was a possibility that her niece hadn't been the victim of a random killer that she relented and told me to drive on over.

The drive gave me an opportunity to assimilate all the information I had so expertly gleaned from the Burris woman. Based on that interview, it was clear that Maureen Wilson had been killed either by Myra Colleridge or by a herd of pissed Catholics. In either case it was because she refused to let pagans play basketball in the Baptist gym. I wondered how Case would react to that information.

Osceola Wilson's house wasn't in Tyler proper. It was located on the outskirts of town on the proverbial red-dirt road. It was a small, three-room frame house sitting on bois d'arc blocks. It was plain, but somehow better kept than I expected. There were several pine trees in the front yard. Each one was encircled by an old truck tire. The tires were painted white and served as flower-bed headers. I don't know what kinds of flowers were in the beds, but they were bright red. There was a dog of indeterminate lineage asleep under the

75

porch. A couple of future Sunday dinners were scratching in the dirt off to the left. The heat was stifling. The dog was probably the smartest life form in the area.

The little house had no air-conditioning, but there were fans in all three rooms. The inside of her house was clean and neat but I noticed the spit can in the corner and the inevitable brown spot on her lip. Osceola was as spry in person as she had sounded over the phone. She was about eighty pounds of leathered skin, gristle, and liver spots. She was the most cantankerous-looking old woman I'd ever seen. That was all right with me.

In all, we talked for about an hour. I enjoyed the conversation. Unfortunately, she didn't have much to add. She confirmed most of what Mrs. Burris had told me. Maureen had led a normal, uneventful life while in Tyler. An above-average student who caused her parents no trouble at all. But Maureen was, according to Osceola, dull to an extreme. When I questioned her about old boyfriends, she said that the Wilson house hadn't been a favorite watering hole for the flat-bellied boys of the area. I pressed her on the subject, and she did remember one boyfriend. His name was Tyrel Counce, and Osceola allowed as they might've gotten married but for the fact that Tyrel was run over and killed by the Dallas-bound Greyhound bus.

She loaned me a picture of Maureen with an explicit understanding that it was to be returned. Judging from the picture, I thought Tyrel might have taken the least painful course.

After graduating from Tyler High School, Maureen attended Tyler Junior College. She earned a certificate in court reporting and worked as a court reporter for two years. All the time she was saving her money to attend East Texas State College. Her dream was to be an English teacher. She got her English degree and taught in an area junior high school for several years until her parents were killed in a house fire. After the fire, she decided to move to Nacogdoches. Osceola said that there were no wealthy family members who might have any money to leave to Maureen. As for enemies, Osceola argued that Maureen hadn't had enough personality to make enemies. But it was clear that she had loved her niece and missed her.

By the time I was ready to go, I think Osceola liked me. She offered me a beer and told me to come on back if I thought of anything else.

It was three-fifteen when I pulled into town. I stopped and called Tommy's. He said that Beth had called to say that she was headed out to Angelina Community College and would meet me later that evening. I passed on lunch and dropped in on Maureen's single love interest.

The residence of Jubal Lee Baker was a tract house about a mile from the college. He ran his taxidermy business out of an attached shop in the back. He was stuffing a goat when I arrived. I didn't ask. Jubal was a short, thick man in his fifties. He was graying and wore glasses. He had a firm handshake and an honest face.

He worked on the goat while we talked. The little room was lined with stuffed animals of varying types. He told me that he'd met Maureen Wilson at church about five years back. The first year he only talked to her between services. After a while, they began to see each other with some regularity. Although he was discreet, Jubal implied that Maureen was much less dull under the right circumstances.

"You don't think I had anything to do with Maureen's murder, do you?" he asked as I was preparing to leave.

"No, Jubal, I don't," I replied.

"She was real strong, you know," he added as if it had just occurred to him.

"What's that?" I asked.

"Maureen was the strongest woman I ever saw," he said. "Once she helped me stuff a horse. Didn't need to hire a helper. She did the liftin' of a man. Whoever killed her had to be real big," he concluded.

On the way to Tommy's I had a picture of Jubal and Maureen stuffing a horse one romantic weekend. The way I figured it, Jubal mounted small animals during the week and Maureen on the weekends.

77

▽

11

A Tough Day

I HEADED BACK TO the office to make a couple of calls. There was a remote possibility that Aunt Osceola hadn't been completely candid with me. I needed to cross-check as much of her information as I could. In my heart, I couldn't see the old girl lying, but my cardiovascular batting average wasn't all that high.

An old friend of mine was the assistant editor for the *Dallas Times*. He had access to the area's most sophisticated computerized information storage and recovery system. Any news item published in the last fifty years was accessed in this system. Chances are that if the Wilson family had been involved in any newsworthy situations in the past, Warren would be able to pull it up on the computer. It would take him about ten minutes to do the research that used to take days.

He wasn't in. I left my name and number and the information I needed. Next I tried Case and met with the same success.

I called maintenance and ordered a portable blackboard for my office. I listed all the information we had about the murder. Sometimes, it's helpful to visualize the elements of a case. Even though there were a number of important pieces of evidence still missing, it would take an extremely myopic cop to view these elements as simply disparate facts. My train of thought was broken by the phone.

"Hey, old stick, it's been a while." The voice on the other end was that of Warren Vandever.

"That it has. What's it been, about a year? Yeah, about a year. How's Dallas?" I asked.

I could hear him talking to someone in his office.

"Hell, things are too damn good to suit me," he said. "I'm ready for the roof to cave in. It just can't be in the cards for me to have a whole year of good luck."

"You're the only silly son of a bitch I know who complains when things are going too well. I think you've become spoiled. If you lived and worked in a hellhole like this, you'd appreciate your situation more. The work is long. The money short. The women are frigid. To tell you the truth, I don't know how much longer I can hold on," I said matter-of-factly.

"Yeah, I got a big picture of that. You're the luckiest son of a gun I know. If a pelican crapped on your head, you'd find a pearl in the shit. It's more likely that you're underworked, overpaid, and reduced to a mere hint of your former self by oversexed, overdeveloped, and farsighted coeds. . . . And I want you to know that I'm jealous as hell. But I'm going to help you out anyway. Although I don't know how much. All I came up with are a couple of obits and two short stories. A JoAnn and Albert Wilson died in a house fire in Tyler and a daughter, Maureen, was murdered out your way a couple of days ago. Everything we have on the murder is from your local police reports. Says here it was a random killing."

"Anything unusual about the house fire that killed the parents?" I asked.

"A simple heater fire," he said.

"Thanks, every little bit of information helps," I added.

There was a pause on the other end. I could almost hear the wheels turning in Dallas. "Is there an angle here worth following up on?" he asked.

I don't like lying to friends, especially helpful ones. In this case, I had to. I couldn't afford to get the *Times* people involved. Leads have a way of disappearing when the investigative traffic gets too busy. Then too, there's always the possibility that whoever had this woman killed was getting pretty relaxed about now. They expected this to go down as a rape and murder by person or persons unknown. An article suggesting more than that in a major paper like the *Times* would have the effect of putting them on guard. It might drive everyone concerned to cover.

"Hell, Warren, anytime there's a murder, there's a story. As far as some special angle, none that I know about. I've got a graduate student who's doing her thesis on investigative reporting techniques and she's using the case as her backdrop," I said as casually as possible.

"You wouldn't bullshit an old bullshitter, would you?" He still sounded a little skeptical.

"I can conceive of situations where I might, but this isn't one of them. But if it'll make you feel better, why not send down a team and I'll let my student follow them around. It'd make a good addition to the paper," I said.

"Let's don't and say we did," he said. He made me promise that if anything interesting developed, I'd let him know. I told him I would.

I just couldn't get a handle on the reason for Maureen Wilson's murder. I was looking out the window and saw Beth coming in the building.

Her entrance was something less than ceremonious. She came in with a look of disgust on her face. She took the chair across from my desk and let out a loud sigh as her body filled the contours.

"This may well be the most frustrating day of my life," she said, tossing her purse to the floor. "I've spent hours talking to scores of people and I've come up with zilch. Tell me that you've fared better," she pleaded.

I couldn't help but smile.

"How tough a case could it be if we solved it in a couple of hours?" I asked softly.

That little piece of wisdom didn't exactly light up her life, but it did make sense to her.

"I guess you're right," she said without enthusiasm.

"Before we call the day a total wash, let's take inventory. Sometimes a solid lead doesn't look that good until all the facts are on the table," I said.

She reached down and took a small notebook from her purse. She got about two sentences in when she suddenly stopped and closed the notebook.

80

"Fowler, I've got to have food. . . . I also need alcohol," she said firmly.

"Never let it be said that Fowler McFarland failed to keep a woman fed," I replied, getting up from the desk.

"I want a great steak and a good white wine," she added.

Her amendment effectively precluded Tommy's. There was a fairly new eatery near the country club. It was called the Chez something or other. With my palate, Tommy's was overspending. However, the thought of some atmosphere and quiet with Beth was pleasant.

The restaurant was very nice. It was a converted old mansion. The seating was in dimly lit nooks and crannies. I'm a nooks man myself. We took a table near a bay window overlooking a small fountain and garden. Beth was starting to show the early warning signs of a smile.

She ordered a prime-cut steak, barely done, and a salad, no dressing. She laid plans for a long siege. She ordered a bottle of expensive imported white wine. The waiter raised his brow at her wine selection. She shot him a look cold enough to freeze his brow permanently. I made a mental note not to fool with this woman when she was in a state of hunger.

With the exception of the wine, I ordered the same.

We talked about our day's labor. Beth had found out that Miss Wilson moved to Nacogdoches fifteen years ago. Never married. She had been active in the community and church and was well thought of at the high school. The principal told Beth that were there more teachers like Maureen Wilson, the state of education in this country wouldn't be in such a mess. As for hobbies, she liked cards with the ladies and rural photography.

"Jesus, Fowler, this was one dull woman," she said as the salad arrived. "I did come up with the name of a man she was seeing from time to time. It was supposedly no big deal according to everyone I talked to. His name is Jubal Lee Baker. Guess what he does for a living?" she challenged.

"Judging from what you've told me about the woman, I'd

guess that Mr. Baker is a taxidermist," I said as if it were a shot in the dark.

"Fowler, you can be an asshole, you know it?" she said while attacking her greens.

"Things like that make me cry on the inside. By the way, what was the purpose of the trip to Angelina Community College?" I asked while trying to find something in my salad that was remotely appetizing.

She rolled her eyes in mild disgust and increased her chewing speed to facilitate the answer.

"I really thought I had something for a while. The reason she was teaching English at the high school was that she'd been fired from Angelina Community College six years ago. Now this woman is just not the type of person to get fired from any job." She paused to finish the salad.

"It turns out that she was fired for not following departmental policy about some technical aspect of court reporting. I talked to the lady who was the chairperson of the department during that period. Her name is Karen Downey. She said that at the time, the college taught a system of notation called the Gregg Symbol System. I gathered it was similar to shorthand. Anyway, our Miss Wilson made changes that she argued improved the system significantly. It was her contention that these changes significantly improved the speed. Evidently the other members of the department didn't share her enthusiasm. They voted to adhere to the original system and directed her to teach only that. Her last year there, she became the mentor for a top-notch court reporting student by the name of Joan Vanhorbeck. The time trials were coming up and the Vanhorbeck girl was a shoo-in to win them. To make a long story short, she used the Wilson system and not only won the trials, but set all-time speed records in doing it. The faculty was less than impressed and voted to have Maureen dismissed. She left court reporting altogether and came to the high school to teach English."

She dropped her shoulders and speculated out loud about whether or not we were on the right track.

"You starting to have some doubts, are you?" I asked as I nibbled at my steak.

"It's just that I can't find any reason for this woman to be murdered. Nothing makes sense in all this," she said dejectedly.

"Don't be so sure. Where does the hotshot court reporter that Maureen trained live now?" I asked.

"Houston, but I don't have an address," she replied.

"Being a court reporter and having a name like Vanhorbeck will make her easy enough to locate," I said.

Beth sat back and looked at me with a curious smile. "What am I missing here?" she asked incredulously. "We're not saying the Vanhorbeck girl hires two professionals to kill Maureen Wilson because she got her disqualified in her time trials, are we?"

There was a slight edge to her voice. She was tired and frustrated and unaccustomed to failure.

"Not exactly," I answered. "Look . . . I got no more than you today. I talked to her oldest and closest relative only to discover that she never did anything of interest in her entire life. She's not in line to inherit anything. She had no lovers to be scorned. She made no enemies of consequence. I talked to the Burris woman. She's the good friend of Miss Wilson who reported the crime. She knew of no motive, period. She did put me onto our taxidermist, Mr. Baker. He was bedding the woman from time to time, but I doubt that a lot of love was involved in the activity. They were simply fate-matched and available."

"Is your lack of success supposed to make me feel better?" she asked.

"Has it ever occurred to you that every motive we eliminate narrows the field? There's an old axiom that says you rule out the impossible, then whatever's left, regardless how improbable, must be the answer. Tonight, we know it wasn't money and it wasn't love. We didn't know that this morning," I argued. I could see some light creeping back into her eyes.

I went on. "The link between Wilson and the Vanhorbeck girl is most of what we've got left. The one out-of-character

83

thing in Maureen Wilson's life to date has been getting fired because of her relationship with this girl. I haven't the foggiest notion what the relationship between the two might be. We need to talk to Vanhorbeck."

"When do you propose we do that?" she asked.

"Before we talk to her, let's have another talk with the head of the court reporting school," I suggested.

"Why don't I give her a call right now?" she suggested, getting up and moving toward the phone.

Working with Beth made me feel good.

"Maybe our luck is changing," she said as she sat back down. "We've got an appointment with Ms. Downey at nine A.M. tomorrow."

"Excellent. Depending on how the meeting goes, let's shoot for a setdown with Vanhorbeck tomorrow evening sometime."

She nodded, and I told her that I needed to stop by my parents' house on the way to Houston.

"You know that you're welcome to meet the folks and have some lunch," I said.

"Probably not a real good idea . . . for a lot of reasons. In fact, let's go in separate cars. I ought to see Anson for a while and I'd just as soon the two of you not meet unless absolutely necessary. He's no fool and, anyway, I'm not a very good liar."

We capped off the meal with a little Blue Bell ice cream while we continued in vain to try and connect the Wilson-Vanhorbeck relationship into a scheme that somehow caused a murder. About nine-thirty we gave up and went back to my house.

We settled on the couch and watched the local news. Only a passing comment about the ongoing investigation of the random killing. That made two times today I'd heard the word "random" used to describe the murder. It bothered me. Somehow, it made the crime seem less significant. However, the lower the profile of the case, the better. Out of sight. Out of mind. Someone might relax and get a little careless.

Beth can get out of her clothes faster than anyone I've ever known. In less than a blink, she was naked and heading for the bedroom. When I caught up with her, she was sitting

Indian style in the middle of the bed. She seemed to be deep in thought as I began to undress.

"Was it the Garcia-Bewis murders that eventually soured you on police work?" she asked. The question caught me off guard. She was still trying to get a fix on me.

"Not entirely," I said without a lot of thought. I lay down on the bed on my back. "In late eighty-four I woke up one morning with no desire to see another crime scene. I didn't want to console another victim, deal with another sleazy informant, or watch the sickening smile of another asshole as he walked freely from a courtroom. It would be fair to say that I'd simply maxed out on the shit associated with the job. It had been coming for some time. If it hadn't been for the Garcia-Bewis case coming along at that time, I probably would've walked away right then."

"What was there about that particular case that kept you going?" she asked.

"I'm not sure. I had a sense of the dimensions of the crime. I thought we were dealing with a psychopath and that meant he probably wasn't insulated. It was just possible that here was a catchable Moriarty. Besides, I knew he wouldn't stop until he was caught. . . . Maybe I just wanted to leave the bureau a winner. . . . I don't know really. At the time the only thing I knew for sure was that a minimum of twenty young boys were missing."

My mind was moving at a rapid pace and flashbacks were coming in waves.

"In your book, you wrote that you were led to that beach by a hunch," she said.

"Both the bureau and the local cops were in agreement that Juan Garcia was a lunatic bisexual who pimped for a wealthy local homosexual named Austin Bewis. Garcia's name came up too many times in the investigations of the various missing boys. We later found out that Garcia would troll the streets in search of vulnerable boys. He'd promise them drugs, money, or shelter if they'd come back to the mansion with him. Once there, they were tied to a large board and sodomized and tortured in unspeakable ways.

Those who were still alive were suffocated with plastic bags. Garcia and Bewis called these sessions board games." I paused for a minute and closed my eyes to shake the visions of those plastic bags from my mind.

"As it turned out, Garcia was suspicious that we were getting close to them. He was very street-smart. Over Bewis's objections, he called a temporary halt to the kidnappings. I was convinced that the key to the investigation lay in the discovery of the bodies. Twenty-some-odd bodies presented a formidable problem for the killers. Bodies are hard to dispose of. One night, it came to me while going through the reports for the umpteenth time. Bewis had spent most of the summers of his youth at his rich aunt's beach house on a fairly remote part of Galveston Island. I knew the bodies were buried somewhere near that beach house. The rest was simple enough. I took a small team down there and located a hardware store where Bewis had purchased several bags of lime. Eventually, using dogs, we located the graveyard. In six hours, we unearthed twenty-two bodies in varying stages of decay."

"It sounds like an incredibly awful experience," she said as she searched my face for reaction.

"Some of the bodies were missing limbs or genitalia. Several still had the plastic bags over the heads." My voice sounded to me to be coldly indifferent. Maybe I'd finally come to terms with that dark portion of my life.

"Nacogdoches makes more sense to me now," she said quietly.

"Garcia got life. Bewis hired a Houston hotshot lawyer and ended up in Rusk. Two years ago, a well-intentioned, underpaid state psychiatrist declared him largely cured of the psychosis that rendered him homicidal in the first place. He was transferred to a private, more comfortable institution. So, in the final analysis, twenty-two young boys are dead and one of the men responsible is being kept alive in Huntsville at taxpayers' expense. The other responsible party is relaxing at a country club sanitarium somewhere in the hill country." I sighed as the last of the day's negative energy escaped from my body.

"That close the loop on your police career?"

"You know something, lady? There are some dark nights when I can't help but deal with those moments again and again. But, I don't want to waste even a minute of the time you're here wallowing in the past. The present is just too damn good," I said as I unraveled her legs and pulled her to me slowly.

Beth didn't say anything. She lay down next to me and curled into my side. I stroked her hair as she fell off to sleep. I discovered that you can make love without sex. I stroked her hair for a long time after she went to sleep. I lay there awhile and thought about Jimmy Wayne and the old man and the young boy.

12

The First Break

A COUPLE OF FEISTY bluejays forced me into a state of consciousness at about a quarter of eight. Beth hadn't moved an inch in the course of the night. I switched off the alarm and quietly made my way to the bathroom.

About halfway through my shave, Beth quietly entered the bathroom. She mumbled something unintelligible, goosed me, and stepped into the shower.

Karen Downey's house was on the way out of town.

As we drove into the neighborhood of nice, middle-class brick homes, I spied a female jogger ahead of me a hundred yards or so. As I drove nearer I became impressed with her lean, athletic legs. She was moving gracefully along, almost effortlessly. I turned into the drive at about the same time the jogger did. She stopped near the front porch and leaned against a support post trying to catch her breath. Beth parked along the curb.

Upon closer inspection, I discovered that the lady was as impressive from the front as she had been from the rear. She was somewhere in her thirties. She was what I used to refer to as a "well-kept secret." That's a woman who works at downplaying her charms. To no avail because the Shadow always knows.

Beth joined me and we approached her.

"Ms. Downey, this is Dr. McFarland from the college," she said.

"Glad to meet you," she said, her chest still heaving a little. "But that's *Miss* Downey. I'm recently divorced," she said as her eyes caught mine for an instant. The distinction wasn't lost on me. Nor, I suspect, was it lost on Beth.

"Why don't we go sit on the back patio and talk while I cool down a little?" she suggested.

The back patio was enclosed by honeysuckle-vined lattice. Karen disappeared for a minute and returned with a pitcher of orange juice.

"Now as I understand it, you want to talk some more about Maureen Wilson," she said, leaning back.

"That's right," Beth said quickly. "We're interested in the period in Miss Wilson's life when she worked for you and the community college."

"I'll tell you anything you want to know, but frankly I'm not real clear on what this is all about. I mean, I thought Maureen was killed by a rapist," she said as she sipped the orange juice.

"Perhaps I can clarify things a little," I said. "The most likely scenario is that Miss Wilson was the victim of a sex offender. However, Mrs. Sheffield and I are doing some background research to rule out other possibilities. Beth is finishing her master's degree in journalism and works for the *Chronicle* on the side. I'm one of the faculty advisers on her thesis and am helping her with her field research."

"I read your book, Dr. McFarland. It was very well written," she said as she placed her empty glass on the table.

"Fowler, please."

"All right," she said with an interesting smile. "What specifically can I help you with?"

"It's our understanding that Miss Wilson was fired while working at the college. Could you elaborate on that situation?" I asked.

"It was an unfortunate situation for everyone concerned," she said, shaking her head. "Maureen was as fine a court reporting instructor as we had. She'd been there about a year when she came to me and told me that she'd modified the symbol system. It's a standardized system very similar to shorthand. She had altered the system fairly dramatically to improve speed. I looked over the new system and was impressed. It was an interesting concept. I took it to the faculty and they rejected it."

"Why?" Beth asked as she paused for a second.

"Some good reasons and some bad. The good related to standardization in the field. We all need to be on the same page in this business. We can't afford for different court reporters to be using different systems. It would cause chaos. Old-timers are afraid of anything that might force them to retool. On the down side, there were some standard jealousies and faculty politics involved," she concluded.

"Did the faculty simply nix the concept outright?" Beth asked.

"No. They voted to set up a committee to look into the matter and called for a review of the committee's findings at the end of one academic year. Maureen was worried that someone else would steal her idea over the course of the year," she said, shaking her head.

"I assume it was about that time that Joan Vanhorbeck got involved," Beth half asked and half stated.

"That's right. Joan was the best student in the program that year. One of the best we've ever had. She idolized Maureen. I believe she saw her as her mentor. Maureen wanted to use her new system at our time trials . . . I guess to show everyone its superiority. The faculty decided that such a plan would be inappropriate. Their argument was that the new system would confuse several of the less skilled candidates. A not completely bogus argument."

"But Maureen ignored the policy and went ahead and used the system anyway . . . is that about it?" Beth asked.

"Well, she taught it to Joan, but no one else. And all hell broke loose when she not only won the trials, but set all-time school records in the process. A number of students complained that since they hadn't been afforded access to the system, they were at an unfair advantage in the trials. A couple of litigations were threatened. I couldn't save Maureen this time. The administration supported her dismissal," she concluded with what seemed to me to be legitimate sadness in her voice.

"What was Maureen's reaction to the decision to fire her?" Beth asked.

"Oh, she still felt that her system had been unfairly evaluated, but I think she realized that her actions were unprofessional. Her pride and her feelings were damaged a little. She was much more accepting of the situation than was the Vanhorbeck girl. She was very vocal, as were her parents."

"So, what happened with respect to the time trials?" Beth asked.

"Joan retook the trials, using the standard system, of course. She won anyway, though with less damage to the records. She graduated number one in the class and moved down to Houston and became a primo reporter. Maureen moved over to the high school and became an English teacher. That's about all I know," she said as she raised her hands in a pose of finality.

"Did you keep up with Maureen or Vanhorbeck after the split?" I asked.

"In a way. Maureen would occasionally come by and we'd have lunch. She would use the opportunity to keep me up to date on the latest success of Vanhorbeck. It was Maureen's way of sort of rubbing our collective noses in the dirt. The last time I talked to Maureen, she was about to go down to Houston and watch Joan work some high-profile trial as I recall," she said.

"Are you saying that the girl was using the new system in Houston?" I asked.

"I don't know for an absolute fact, but that's my impression," she said.

"Well, that about does it for me," I said as I got up.

"Are you a runner?" she asked with a smile.

"Not if alternative transportation is available," I replied as we left.

We drove around the block and I pulled over. Beth pulled up next to me and didn't get out of her car. I got out and walked to her window.

"Are you a runner?" she asked in her deepest, most exaggeratedly sensuous voice.

"Come on now. You need to take the question in the spirit in which it was posed," I said. "I'm sure distance running can get pretty lonely."

"Right. Why don't you get a scooter and follow along behind her and keep her company?" she asked with more than a little edge in her voice.

"I've decided to reserve my conditioning procedures to those which I can pursue with you," I said with my most conciliatory tone.

"Deal," she said, smiling. "I'll see you at three P.M. in the lobby of the *Chronicle* building," she said as she drove off in the direction of Houston.

After getting some gas, I started south as well. I figured it would take about an hour and a half to get to my parents' house. That assumed that I didn't encounter any difficulties along the way. That strip of highway is notorious for speed traps. Some of the quaint hamlets that line the interstate are prone to issue inordinate numbers of traffic citations, mostly to folks with out-of-state plates. They are not above, however, issuing them to in-state travelers when the economic need arises. The towns consider the speed traps a creative form of revenue enhancement. Their constabularies are not known for their hospitality or their commitment to due process. The most infamous of these places is a pustule named Diboll. That's pronounced as if it refers to a sterility condition in males. I always figure that if I can make it through Diboll unscathed, I'm home free.

13

Back to Houston

Aʙᴏᴜᴛ ᴛᴇɴ-ᴛᴡᴇɴᴛʏ ɪ ᴘᴜʟʟᴇᴅ into the drive of my parents' house. They have a beautiful yard. There must be thirty varieties of roses and huge hydrangea bushes line the walk. They have the bluest flowers I've ever seen. My mother says the shade of blue is related to the amount of acidity in the soil. Dad claims it is due to the neighbor's dogs pissing in the flower beds.

It would probably be a typical Saturday cookout. A lot of barbecue. A lot of beer. A lot of porch sitting. I could tell from Dad's general demeanor that he was several Miller Lites into the day when I got there.

The McFarland family hadn't exactly been the Cleavers, but we did all right. My folks are simple people with a strong sense of family. They always provided as much support as they were capable of giving. It hadn't always been pretty, but it'd always been there.

Mom was bringing a load of ribs to be grilled and I recalled my first birthday party. I had just turned six and my mother had invited the neighborhood rug-rats over to celebrate the occasion. It was to be held on a Saturday, and because my father had been known to tie one on from time to time, Mom expressly warned him to avoid showing up during the party in a drunken condition. At about three o'clock, at the peak of the festivities, Dad's truck pulled up and he literally fell out. He staggered up to the crowd of kids and wished me a happy birthday. Having done that, he promptly passed out in the backyard. He was just lying there when my mother threw a tablecloth over his prostrate frame and set the birth-day cake on top of him. We all gathered around the human table and blew out the candles. The kids thought it was great. I was probably the only kid in the world whose father doubled as a piece of furniture for special occasions. Later Mom was pissed. Dad was apologetic. I was confused. We all survived, none the worse for wear.

"Son, I've got three or four of the Hollywood ribs without sauce. Go in there and give your mother a hug and then come on back and tell me what's going on," he said, busily turning the meat. He was in good spirits.

My mother never changes. She gave me a hug and asked about the college. She had heard about the murder on the news and mentioned it in passing. I remained mute on the subject. She told me that she had given up beer and that Dad had given up smoking. I've always thought that balancing vices within a family is a good idea. She warned me that a couple of aunts and their families were going to drop by later. In their younger days these get-togethers always ended in marathon penny-ante poker games. Nowadays, the afternoon ends with all present becoming couch potatoes.

Mom, Dad, and I ate an early dinner, and they filled me in on all the relatives. I learned who was still alive and who wasn't. One of my cousins was about to marry for the fourth time. A distant cousin had been sent to prison for drug-related crimes. My grandmother, now nearing eighty, was in the hospital again. Once caught up on the latest workings in the family, I excused myself and told them I had a meeting in Houston. Dad called me a butthole for leaving him to deal with all the relatives alone.

I couldn't have timed my escape any better. I hit a crease in the Houston traffic and made it to the meeting place right on time. Beth and I met at the door.

"How are things on the home front?" she asked as we entered.

"Some things never change. The McFarland household is one of those constants. And the Sheffield household?" I asked.

"Copacetic, thank you," she said as we walked to the elevators.

I knew that Lion would be at his desk. It was a Saturday

afternoon with the Astros in town. Chris had always worked those Saturdays when the ball team was in town. He told me he got more done when the place was near empty. A creature more true to his established habits I had never known.

True to form, he was working away. Chris looked like someone who worked for a newspaper. His sleeves were rolled up, his glasses were on top of his head, and as always he had a pencil behind his ear. I introduced Beth, using her married name. He shot me a quick little look as his glasses nestled back on his nose. He caught the name immediately but made no comment beyond polite salutations. He's always been a player.

"We're in town doing a little one-day research on a local story up in Nacogdoches. We'd appreciate it if you'd pull up what you have on a Miss Joan Vanhorbeck. She's been a court reporter here for several years," I said, giving him all the leads I could.

"Looking for anything in particular?" he asked as he punched up the name on the terminal nearest him.

"At the very least, an address," I said. "But I'll take anything else you can find."

"Well, you know the phone company publishes a book with all the addresses and phone numbers of area residents," he said with a little acid in his tone.

I ignored the shot and hoped he'd have more than an address.

"Well, well, well," he mumbled as he read the printout. "I guess it's just as well you didn't use the phone book. Your Miss Joan Ellen Vanhorbeck has recently become a crime statistic. She was murdered six days ago," he said matter-of-factly.

Beth's reaction was immediate. She shot me a look of restrained excitement. She knew that the probabilities of these two women being killed within days of one another by coincidence were minuscule. We were on the trail of something. I asked Chris to give me a copy of everything the *Chronicle* had run on the killing. There was the initial news story and a smaller follow-up piece. Other than the obit, that

95

was it. Beth and I read them together. Both women were raped and murdered. Both women were strangled. Joan had been choked with her pantyhose. I liked flexibility in a killer. The follow-up story simply echoed the normal police excuse about sex crimes being among the most difficult to solve. The obit gave the address of her parents. They lived in an older suburb of Houston called Bellaire. We thanked Chris for his help and made for the door.

Once in the elevator, Beth was unable to conceal her enthusiasm any longer. "This has got to be the break we've been looking for," she yelped. "There is no possible way that these two killings are coincidence," she added.

"Where do we go from here?" I asked.

You could see the wheels turning again. She prefaced her answer with an approval-seeking expression. "We interview the parents and try to see what these two women had in common that got them killed," she said.

"That's not bad, lady. If you're not careful, someone's going to mistake you for a reporter," I said. "However, before we talk to the parents, let's see what else we can find out about the murder of the Vanhorbeck woman," I suggested.

"And, of course, you know someone on the police force who will assist us in that," she said with a smile.

"I just might," I replied. "Let's find a couple of pay phones and get busy. You call the Vanhorbecks and set up the interview as soon as possible. I'll call an old friend of mine on the force and see if he will help us."

Danny Allusoto was a good friend and one of the best homicide detectives in Houston. Unfortunately, he wasn't on duty that afternoon. He was on his way out when the phone rang. He was glad to hear from me, but had plans for the evening. I told him I needed the official reports on the killing. He was willing to help but wanted to meet on Monday. I finally convinced him of the need for a "right now" meeting. He agreed to meet us at James's Coney Island near Main Street downtown. It was a good place. They had the best chili dogs in the world.

Beth informed me that we had an appointment to meet

with the Vanhorbecks the next morning at ten o'clock. I was impressed. I took a route that cut through Bellaire. We made a note of the Vanhorbeck residence.

"I thought for a minute that they weren't going to allow us over. I had to tell them that we were on the trail of their daughter's killer," she said.

We'd been at a table about five minutes when Danny walked in carrying a manila envelope. We got up and met him at the counter, then all got in line and loaded up on the house specialty. I think their secret lies in the chili. We sat down and proved the theory that there is no polite way to eat a chili dog.

In the course of the meal chatter, it became obvious to me that Danny was more interested in Beth than the reason for the meeting. It was clear to me that he had fallen in love. It was clear because I'd seen him do it twenty or thirty times before. In Allusto's case, his heart was circumcised.

I read the police reports while he invested in Beth. I decided that Beth could handle herself. He took aim and gave it his best shot. Beth was wonderful. Just interested enough to keep his attention and just distant enough to leave herself an out. She had done this before. Danny was uncharacteristically overmatched.

Allusoto eventually caught on to her scam. Never one to dally in the face of defeat, he turned his attention back to me.

"So what is all the concern over your basic 'single-girl-gets-killed-by-pervert' case?" he asked with the insensitivity of a twenty-year cop.

The deceiving of newspaper types is an entirely different proposition from deceiving the police. I don't like doing the first and I don't do the second.

"I gather from your tone that this is an open-closed case," I said. He nodded. "Earlier this week," I continued, "a woman was attacked and killed in Nacogdoches. The two women, ours in Nacogdoches and the Vanhorbeck woman, knew each other. There are also a number of similarities in the killings. Both women were strangled with a piece of their underwear. Both women appeared to have been raped, but no seminal fluids were present. Both killings were slick."

Danny's instincts and experience took over from his hormones. He told me that another detective had been working this case and that we ought to get him into our investigation.

"Hell, you know that if I turn up anything of consequence I'll get in touch," I said. "All I've got are a few theories. I'm keeping a low profile so as not to attract the press. Right now the killers don't know that someone has made the connection between the two murders. I need to keep it that way."

He wrote the name of the detective on the folder. He took a last drink from his beer and told me to lose the folder somewhere. He knew that he could count on me to get the department involved at the right time.

As he left, Beth asked if I thought we could trust him to keep this quiet.

"You can trust Danny Allusoto with anything but your virtue. It wouldn't matter though. We had to tell him regardless of his discretion. He's the law. Forget any bullshit you might've heard about concealing information from the police. The most important thing about any criminal investigation is solving it and locking up the responsible miscreants. The best chance of doing that rests with the police." She was a little taken aback by the intensity of my reaction. "Hey, I don't mean to be so damn obdurate, it's just that the story should never take precedence over catching the criminal," I added.

Beth nodded and looked at her watch. "Fowler, I need to be home tonight. I'll meet you in the morning in front of the house," she said with what I hoped was a bit of remorse in her voice.

"Let's make it the little donut shop around the corner from the Vanhorbeck house about nine-thirty. And lady . . . we all do what we need to do. Then we make the best of the rest," I said, getting up. I gave her a kiss and drove her back to her car.

$\triangledown$

14

The Plot Thickens

THE NIGHT WAS LONG and largely sleepless. When I was finally able to put a few minutes of solid sleep together, they were interrupted by the hotel wake-up call. I turned on the radio and started to clean up. I was informed that the comfort index was at a dangerous level this morning. I gathered from the weatherman that the comfort index was the relationship between temperature and humidity. These two in combination can cause a lot of heatstroke in a town the size of Houston. I thought the name of the index odd. I could never remember being comfortable while outside in Houston. At least not in the summer months. If I were running a radio station, I think I'd run pollution, crime, and traffic through a computer with temperature and humidity and come up with what I'd call the morbidity index. Let all the listeners know what the odds of their surviving another day in Houston really were.

When I got to the donut shop, Beth was waiting for me. She hugged me real tight. It was more than a nice-to-see-you hug. We took my car to the interview.

The Vanhorbeck home was large and expensive. We were met at the door by a smallish, balding man in his fifties. Even with his slight stature and watery blue eyes, there was something strong about him. He introduced himself as Jack Vanhorbeck. He showed us to a living area where we were introduced to Mrs. Vanhorbeck. Dana Vanhorbeck was built on a line with her husband. She was poised and very controlled. Her mouth turned down in a constant frown and her eyes were lifeless. This was an unhappy woman.

She served iced tea. The inside of the house was right out

of *Better Homes and Gardens*. . . . Without looking, I was sure I didn't have a Goofy glass. I felt uncomfortable.

"I insisted that we have you here," the wife said. "My husband and I share a mutual pain, but we deal with it differently. His medication is time and distance. Jack is convinced that eventually time will heal the wounds and stop the pain of Joni's murder." The look in her eyes was the coldest I've ever seen. I wondered if she had been like this before the murder. She shifted her gaze to a set of table pictures. They were of her daughter. One was a baby picture and the other was a graduation shot. "Time won't heal my pain," she continued. "I need to know . . . to see . . . to feel her killer punished. I want to be a part of his suffering. I want to see his eyes when he hears the sentence." During the entire monologue her voice was unchanged. There had been no deviation in pitch, rate, or volume. This wasn't the typical outburst of an outraged parent. It was calm and calculated. I believe that Dana Vanhorbeck was capable of cutting the throat of her daughter's killer. I know that occasionally a person covers up stress by being abnormally calm. I think she was in complete control.

She and her husband provided an interesting role reversal. I've encountered revenge-seeking fathers before. I've seen mothers rendered passive by the death of their children, but this combination of reactions was new to me.

Beth's eyes never left the woman. I hoped that she was composed enough to be tough and probative. Those doubts were quickly erased when she calmly took out her recorder and placed it on the cocktail table. She opened her notebook and switched on the recorder.

"I've never lost anyone close to me in such a violent and cruel manner. I don't know how you feel. I couldn't," she said. "We are, however, very sorry for your loss. Anything we find that might help catch those responsible for your daughter's death will go straight to the police." Jack came over and sat down beside Dana. He put his hand on her knee. I felt a lot of compassion for the man. He had not only lost a daughter, he was on the brink of losing a wife as well. Hate and bitterness can kill as effectively as a weapon.

"Frankly, I've given up hope of finding the person responsible for Joan's death," Dana said, focusing on Beth. "I know it's just been a week, but the police told us that random sex crimes are very hard to solve and not to get our hopes up. I understand that less than one-third of these types of murders are ever solved. The police don't seem very motivated. I'm just happy that someone still cares enough to keep investigating."

"Actually, we're investigating two murders," Beth offered. "Earlier this week, a woman by the name of Maureen Wilson was murdered in Nacogdoches. The similarities between the two killings are several. Add to that the fact that your daughter and Maureen Wilson knew each other, and the random concept gets frail. Once random is gone, motive provides a trail to the killer."

The news of Maureen Wilson's death brought an immediate change in Jack's posture and attitude. He was visibly shaken by the news. Mrs. Vanhorbeck mumbled something about trying unsuccessfully to contact Miss Wilson earlier in the week.

Given their reaction, I thought it best to fill them in on our investigation. I was brutally frank and told them about our suspicions with respect to hired killers and staged rapes.

Jack's pragmatic mind was processing the information while Dana talked to us. She told us that Joan and Maureen had been close friends while Joan was in Nacogdoches. According to her, Miss Wilson had been the only teacher in the department who realized her daughter's potential. She mentioned that she had taught Joan a new notation system that greatly enhanced her speed. She reiterated what Karen Downey told us.

Beth asked them about any enemies their daughter might have had. They agreed that Joan had been far too passive and yielding to inspire hate or aggression. She sounded remarkably like a young Maureen Wilson.

Jack pointed out that the relationship between Joan and Maureen hadn't ended with Joan's graduation from college and move to Houston. They corresponded with some regularity. I asked if the letters were available. Neither of them had any idea where they might be, but Dana promised to look through Joan's papers to see if she could find them.

"This is going to sound strange," Jack said. "But all of this has to somehow be connected to the Costillo trial."

Dana said she didn't see the connection. Beth picked up on the new scent and asked Jack to explain.

"Paco Costillo is the son of a very powerful Mexican drug lord. Three years ago, the boy and a couple of his bodyguards were entertaining a hooker in their room at a downtown hotel. They killed the girl and tried to dispose of the body. They wrapped her in a blanket and were carrying it down the stairs when they ran into a family coming up the stairs. It was late and the elevators were temporarily down. The prosecution argued that the family must've noticed something wrong, because the Costillo people killed all three of them. There was a man, his wife, and their five-year-old daughter. Somehow, they got all four bodies to a van, took them to the outskirts of town, and buried them in a shallow grave near Sugarland. The next day, a teenager hunting nutria for bounty spotted a foot sticking up from the grave. The police tied it all together in a matter of hours. The evidence was convincing, but Esteban Costillo would probably still have gotten his boy off but for one detail. It was K. Brad Turrow's son and his family who had been slain."

He stopped to wipe his eyes and drink some tea. The mentioning of Turrow's name started my wheels rolling. I had been out of the country at the time of the killing and the trial. Consequently, I knew scant few of the specifics of the case. I remember being impressed with Turrow and his efforts in penal reform, given that his family had been victimized. This was an interesting turn of events.

"Turrow took a personal interest in the investigation. He offered a million-dollar reward for information leading to the conviction of those responsible. He applied so much political pressure that even Esteban couldn't extricate his boy from the mess. They even hired Sercy Gorman to defend the boy.

102

As good as Sercy was, the best he could do was get him life. Given the nature of the crime, that in itself was a miracle. Turrow was furious. He demanded the death penalty. It was Joan's first major criminal case. Dana and I attended every session. Miss Wilson came down during the trial and helped Joan with her transcriptions. She attended a number of the sessions."

"Where is the connection?" Beth asked.

"I don't have a solid reason. My instincts tell me there must be a connection. It's intuitive. There was so much evil in that courtroom. In the face of all they had done, even during the coroner's vivid descriptions of the dead child, there wasn't a hint of compassion, much less contrition, in the faces of those animals." He spoke with conviction.

Jack Vanhorbeck was a bright man. Plus I'd played a few hunches in my time. My instincts were talking to me too. Before Beth could ask another question, I reminded her that we had another appointment this morning and were running a little late. She didn't miss a beat. She confirmed my bogus appointment and we went about the business of tying up loose ends.

"I should caution you," I said, "about revealing any of your suspicions about the Costillo trial and the murder to anyone else. In the first place, it's too speculative for the police to buy into. Secondly, if you're on to something and word reaches the street, everything will dry up."

"But this might be just the lead the police need to get back into the investigation with some energy," Jack said.

"Folks, the police department has a number of leaks. The wrong people in the department having access to this information, should it prove true, could even put us all in danger. We've already told a high-ranking, reliable detective about the two murders and their similarities. We'll pass on your suspicions about the Costillo trial," I assured them.

They agreed to wait awhile and see what progress was made in the case.

Back in the car, Beth was curious about the rush to leave. I told her that I knew the motive for the killings and probably the killer as well. We drove through a Burger King and headed for the nearest motel. Beth took a chair, unwrapped a burger, and started to eat. She was patiently awaiting my explanation.

"Joan and Maureen were murdered as part of a plan to get Paco Costillo out of prison," I said as I scraped the tomatoes off my burger. "Maureen creates a new system of notation. She teaches it to Joan. She's fired and teaches it to no one else. Joan comes to Houston and works the Costillo trial. Paco is convicted. Now begins the appellate process. What do you suppose happens if all the transcripts of the original trial are missing? That would leave only the original notes of the court reporter. Since they're taken in a unique notation system understood by only two people in the world, the logical course of events is to eliminate those two people. I'm not a lawyer, but I'll bet that such a scenario at the appellate level might result in retrial or even dismissal."

"That's got to be it. It all fits and nothing else does," she said, ready to explode.

"The man behind the killings figures to be Esteban Costillo, and he won't allow two nosy people to dig around and expose the plan. The moment he suspects that we're trying to shit in his nest, he'll be on us like ugly on an ape," I warned.

"I thought those people avoided killing cops and reporters," she said.

"Lady, we're not reporters or cops. We're meddlers. Besides, the Costillo types will kill anyone who gets in their way. No one is immune from them. Not the police, not politicians, and certainly not us. They're too rich and too insulated to fear the system. Hell, they're a waste product of the system."

"What are you suggesting that we do?" she asked with some reservation in her tone.

"I'm not sure. I just don't want to expose you to any unnecessary risks," I replied.

"The business comes with risks," she said. "Hell, it's probably too late to worry about it now. We've already asked a lot of questions of a lot of people. They couldn't afford to leave me alone. They don't know how much I know or don't know. So if you're thinking about sending me somewhere while you continue, don't," she said firmly.

"All right, but keep something in mind. From this point on you need to do exactly what I tell you. If I get the impression that you're not treating this with sufficient caution, I'll close it down. Deal?" I asked.

"That works for me," she said as she started to undress. In a matter of seconds she was standing before me clad only in a form-fitting baby-blue teddy. I held my ground.

"One of the best things about our relationship up till now has been that the sex has been uncomplicated. It begins and ends with pleasure. Your motives have always been clear to me. I don't want to wonder whether or not you're with me for pleasure or gratitude."

She slowly started to loosen my belt. "When I want to express my gratitude, I send thank-you cards. I never confuse my motives where sex is concerned—never," she said looking me in the eye.

I figured that I'd made my point with about as much conviction as I could muster. A man needs to know his limitations.

About five o'clock I asked her about her plans for the remainder of the evening. She told me that she was to have dinner with Anson at eight.

"That'll work. I've got to do a little legwork before we get back to Nacogdoches," I said. "There are a couple of people I probably ought to see tonight."

"What kind of legwork?" she asked.

"I'd feel better with a legal opinion with respect to our theory. I've a friend who used to be a judge who should be able to clarify that for us. I also want to know as much as possible about the Costillo family. Then I need to find out about the existence of official trial transcripts and their location. I've a friend in the FBI who ought to be able to fill me in a little."

"Can't we do some of that legwork together tomorrow

sometime?" she asked. "I'd like to be there myself."

"I best meet with my friend in the FBI alone. I think a good time for that would be tonight over dinner. However, tomorrow would probably be a good time to meet with our legal expert. What's a good time for you tomorrow?" I asked.

"I don't know. Let's negotiate in the shower," she said, pulling me in the direction of the bathroom.

Personally I've always been a believer in cleanliness. You know, next to godliness and all that. I also believe that showering alone is dangerous. Consequently, I believe that showers should be tandem affairs. In devising my theory on shower hazards I hadn't factored in Beth. Thirty minutes later I crawled from the bathroom, clean but crippled.

I called Kermit Greenburg. He was the ranking FBI wizard on the Gulf Coast. I hoped to talk him into having a drink somewhere and doing a little informal probing of his information-filled mind.

The Costillo people scared the hell out of me. I needed as much information about them and their habits as I could get. Information is power. Finding Kermit might prove difficult. He gave new meaning to eccentric. He wasn't a womanizer or a carouser. He was likely to be in Galveston taping the sound of the tide coming in or a mullet farting during a full moon.

"Fowler," Beth said as she paused near the door, "couldn't a professional code decipherer translate the notes?"

"Possibly, maybe probably," I said, thinking about her question. "But in the first place, I doubt the notes will ever be found. In the second place, the only two people that for sure could translate are dead. Thirdly, courts are very wary of exotic complications and the Sercy Gormans of the world are very good at convincing appellate panels that such confusion mitigates his client's due process rights."

"This is some weird shit," she said as she left.

I got Kermit's answering machine. I was in the process of leaving him a message when he broke in. "Fowler, what are you doing in town?" he asked with his thick nasal twang.

"I'm here to eat, drink, and get informed," I said. "Do you

know how much you sound like Howard Cosell on the phone?"

"No . . . I never talked to Howard on the phone, but you're a real sweetheart to mention it. I wish I had his money and I'm sure he wishes he had my personality and charm. Where are you?" he asked.

"I'm at the Holiday Inn off the six-ten loop and two-ninety," I answered.

"How about Louie's at eight o'clock?" he suggested.

"You got a date, you savage," I said and hung up.

The restaurant was located on Clear Lake about an hour away.

Houston can be a beautiful city and evenings are the best time to get out and about. I took Memorial Drive to town. It winds through one of the wealthiest areas in town. Some of the largest oaks in the world are along this drive. Joggers were out in force. I took the Pierce elevated to get the view of the skyline at twilight.

A few miles from the restaurant I was forced to take the Gulf Freeway. It's always busy and the speeds range between thirty-five and eighty-five miles an hour. Lanes are viewed as meaningless. The faster drivers treat the highway as if it were an Alpine event. I got into the far right lane and tried to survive.

Kermit pulled in as I was getting out of the car. "I see that you still have a weakness for sports cars," he said, looking over the Corvette.

"And I see that you still have no desire to own a real car," I said. "Besides, my affinity for sports cars is a strength, not a weakness."

Kermit was driving his usual General Motors version of the generic automobile. The color was indescribable and not found in nature. He didn't look like an FBI agent. He looked more like a Jewish businessman. He was balding with a prominent nose. He was short and not exactly a physical specimen. I doubt that he could bench-press *War and Peace*. At first impression, he was easy to underestimate, and that was a major mistake. I was with him when he shot and killed two armored-car robbers on a downtown street. He is quietly fearless, coldly competent, and extremely knowledgeable in his field. He doesn't work to live, he lives to work. I was sure that he could help me figure out the best course of action with respect to Costillo.

We were seated at a window table. There were several boats moored at the restaurant's pier. They'd come by sea to dine. I'd always wanted to come here by boat.

"I'm involved in a sticky murder investigation," I said. "It started out as a piss-ant killing in Nacogdoches. I decided to use it as a vehicle for a good student's master's thesis. The more we dug into it, the more complicated it became. I came to Houston to interview a young woman who knew the victim. I discovered that she had been murdered as well. I think these two women were killed because they might have queered the plans of Esteban Costillo to get his son Paco released from prison."

Kermit had been steadily eating while I was talking. He had been listening attentively the whole time, but the mention of Costillo intensified his interest. He took it all in without comment.

"I need anything you have that might help me put this together," I said. "I know I'm on the right track, but right now all I've got are theories and disjointed facts. I can't go to court with what I've got now."

"I don't know how it'll play in court, but it'll sure as hell sell a million paperbacks," he said, sitting back in his chair. "If anybody else in the world told me this story, I'd dismiss it as imagination. However, I learned a long time ago that it's unwise to underestimate your instincts. Assuming that you're correct in all of this, the first thing you need to do is watch your ass. These particular people are the most ruthless vipers I've ever encountered. They wouldn't hesitate to kill you. Over the last six or seven years the Costillos have been responsible for a couple of hundred hits. They are not bothered by boundaries or custom in their carnage. We're sure it was on orders from Esteban that a judge in Plano was killed. He had a reputation for being tough in drug cases.

They tried for a change of venue. They were turned down. During a recess, the judge was found in the restroom. His head was still in the toilet where he had drowned in his own waste. And you're treading on much more dangerous ground than that judge. The old man adores the kid. He will do anything to protect him. As best I've been able to figure out, Paco is the only thing in this world that Esteban loves. He had three sons at one time. The other two were casualties of his rise to power in the drug world. I guess you could call them dues."

This was pretty much consistent with Jack Vanhorbeck's assessment of the situation. It confirmed my worst fears and made me regret allowing Beth to stay involved.

Kermit went on to tell me a number of interesting things about the players in the case. It seems that K. Brad Turrow had become convinced early in the case that Paco would somehow escape justice. He hired at least two sets of killers to take Paco out. In both cases, the hitters were taken out before they could fill the contract. Even after his conviction and life sentence, there were a couple of additional attempts on the kid's life. One took place in prison and the other on the way to an appeals hearing. Again, the hitters were unsuccessful. The Mexican Mafia is very powerful down here now. Turrow was aware that a life sentence meant only about eight to ten served years before parole was possible.

"Why not just take out Turrow?" I asked.

"My guess is that he would've, had he no other options. Hitting Turrow would be very bad for business. It would have to be a last-resort hit. It's my feeling Turrow was warned that any additional efforts would result in the death of members of his family or business associates. The attempts stopped." Kermit ordered a pitcher of margaritas.

"If I'm right about all this, I can't afford to ask too many more questions," I said. "The word will get back to Costillo and I'll be dead. If I go to the police with what I have, they won't be able to do anything, but one of Costillo's ears in the department will get word back to him and I'm dead again.

109

I don't have enough to go anywhere with it and I'd hate the taste of eating it."

"I agree with most of that. I wouldn't go near the HPD with any of this. I also wouldn't do any more nosing around here. It doesn't look to me like you have a lot of options. It might just be that you'll have to cultivate new tastes," he said, lifting his glass in mock toast.

"Anything the bureau can do?" I asked.

"Aside from warning some folks to guard the transcripts, not much I can do. Very little of what you've laid out falls into our jurisdiction. I don't have to tell you that local murders are local affairs. We're only interested in Paco as a means to get at the old man. The Turrow murders didn't really have anything to do with the family business, which does fall into our territory. It was a simple case of a young college kid having some fun killing people on the weekend. If I can figure a way to tie your situation in to our investigation, I will. I firmly believe that the best way to Esteban is through the boy. But I doubt we'll turn up anything on the plot to get Paco out. The old man knows we've got him under constant watch. He'll have these arrangements taken care of outside normal channels. One thing's for sure. He'll stop at nothing to get the boy back. . . . Have you ever seen the old man?" he asked.

"No, I don't think I have," I answered.

"He's not like any Mexican I've ever seen. He's in his sixties with silver hair and a dark complexion. He wears a patch over his left eye. His right eye is incredibly green. He has no left hand. I've never seen him smile and he's got the coldest look I've ever seen."

I thought to myself that Mrs. Vanhorbeck might be his match with respect to physical sinisterism. I sat back and watched the last vestiges of daylight cast a pink hue across the lake. The few clouds were a shade that artists call Haynes gray. Why wasn't I on one of those boats, concerned only with surviving another tryst with Beth?

"Want my best advice?" he asked. I didn't respond. I knew I was going to get it one way or the other. "Reel in your line

110

and go back to Nacogdoches. Don't tell the police, don't ask any more questions, and don't write about it anywhere. Call Allusoto and tell him it was a dead end. Select another subject for your student's thesis. Get into your car and get the hell out of here while you still can."

"That what you'd do in my shoes?" I asked without looking away from the sunset.

"Yeah, that's what I'd do," he said after a pause.

We ordered another pitcher of poison. I joined him this time. We invested an hour or so in pleasant areas of conversation. Kermit was good company. The last thing he told me was that he would make some discreet inquiries about the Paco situation and get back to me.

▽

15

All Problems Big and Small

I WASN'T SLEEPY, SO I drove around for a while. I parked the car just inside the entrance to Herman Park. This is Houston's version of Central Park. It's really a pretty area. It was a clear, clean night. I pushed myself up out of the seat to the back of the car and sat there for a while. To the right were the Mecom Fountains. To the left were the ivy-covered walls of Rice University. I could see the distant lights of the zoo and the planetarium. A few feet away a couple of college kids were entangled under a huge oak tree. This was a perfect night for lying under an oak tree with a fair-haired lass.

I wondered where Beth was about now. Mostly I wondered if she was wondering.

Kermit's advice had been good. Just being right doesn't count for much in court. This wasn't a new lesson for me, but it might be for Beth. I wasn't sure she would understand. Then there was the question of Costillo getting away with killing several people. As desensitized as my years in the business had made me, it still galled me to think of letting him walk away from this. Worse still, his vile offspring would be loosed upon society to keep the family sociology intact. What would I say to the Vanhorbecks? Overshadowing all of the considerations was Beth. I wasn't sure I could do anything that would reduce me in her eyes. How much risk was I opening her up to? Shit, what about Case? His election was near and I'd left him out on a limb. This was a real major-league cluster fuck. Now I remembered why I got out of this business in the first place.

I couldn't just walk away from it. I decided to do three things immediately. First, I'd call Allusoto and stall him.

Second, Beth and I would find out if the court reporting theory would float. Tomorrow's interview ought to clarify that once and for all. Last and most important, if I couldn't accumulate enough evidence to take to the police or to the press, I'd take what I had to K. Brad Turrow. He was the only player in all this with enough horsepower to take on Costillo.

I was about to slide back into the seat and leave when the young man under the tree yelled over and asked the time. I told him it was nearing midnight. If he was smart he wouldn't worry too much about the time. There are too few trees in a man's life as it is.

Beth was waiting for me at the Denny's near my motel. We talked about some of the things Kermit had told me. I omitted part of it. This wasn't the time or place. I called Danny from the pay phone at the restaurant. He was swamped with caseload and didn't press me at all about contacting him later on the subject of the Vanhorbeck killing.

"Lady, it's time to see one Nancey Jean Love, formerly Judge Nancey Jean Love, and now professor of law at the University of Houston," I said, taking her by the hand.

It was starting to drizzle a little. The clouds were moving in and the forecast was dreary. The main campus of the University of Houston is architecturally eclectic. Most of the buildings are white stone with red-tile roofs. They're the original buildings of the campus. The newer buildings are more modern edifices. There is a good balance between the old and the new. Throw in a couple of hundred old oak trees and set the entire facility in the middle of one of Houston's raunchiest ghettos, and you've captured the essence of the school.

When I first met Nancey, she was a law student. I'd been invited to a forum on campus to discuss the First Amendment as it related to protecting news sources from the bureau perspective. She was scary bright. She graduated at the top of her class and practiced in the area for a few years until she accepted an appointment to a judgeship created by the death of the elected judge. Later she ran for and won the office. She

113

held the position for several years. Four or five years ago she decided that the classroom was where her heart was. We had an eleven o'clock appointment.

She was waiting in the outer office when we arrived. She hadn't changed much. "Fowler, it's so good to see you again," she said with a Southern drawl that would rival Case's. "I was just this minute tellin' Joelle about the talk you gave on the First Amendment. Do you remember? It was a most interestin' departure from the mainstream views of the day. . . . Oh, I'm sorry. Here I am ramblin' on and I've not been introduced to your friend," she said, extending her hand.

I introduced Beth, using her married name. I told Nancey of her thesis and our investigation. I explained that we had a small legal question of a hypothetical nature.

"Haven't we met before?" Nancey asked Beth as she searched her memory for the time and place.

"It's possible," Beth said smiling. "I live in Houston with my husband, Anson Sheffield."

"That's it, of course. I've seen you with Anson at a function somewhere. Maybe the art show last week," Nancey said, relieved to have placed Beth.

"That's probably it. We were there," Beth pointed out.

"You're a very lucky woman," she said with a wry look. "Anson was the catch of the town."

"That's what he tells me," Beth said as they both laughed.

I don't know when I'd had so much fun. For some strange reason, I felt compelled to get on with business, so I broke in when they paused to take a breath.

"Our question is this. If a convicted criminal were to file an appeal for a new trial and the court records of the original trial were lost or destroyed, what effect would their loss have on the appeal?"

Nancey took off her glasses and tapped them against the side of her head. I liked people who thought things through before they spoke.

"The answer is simple enough. Constitutionally speaking, every person has the right to a fair trial and therefore an

114

appeal based on the fairness of the original trial. As you know, appeals are largely predicated upon procedural issues and not matters of guilt or innocence as such. These procedures are only documentable through the trial transcripts. There have been a few cases where the official transcripts were lost or destroyed, let's say by fire, and the appeals court had no recourse but to release the incarcerated party. Those situations have been eliminated in recent years. In Texas there are three official copies of the transcripts and an audio tape of the transcripts is made as well. This is standard procedure in major felonies and capital cases. So there is no real chance for all the transcripts to be lost," she concluded.

"Where are the various official copies kept?" Beth asked as she read my mind.

"One copy is kept at the courthouse of origin. One copy is filed with the prosecuting attorney's office, and a third copy is filed with the state repository of trial records. That happens to be right here on campus in the law library. The tape also stays with the DA's office. And don't forget the original notes of the court reporter. The court can always have them produce another transcript if necessary." Nancey looked confident that we finally understood the unlikelihood of our hypothetical situation ever materializing.

"Bottom line . . . if the records were lost completely, the convicted person gets off?" I asked.

"You are nothing if not persistent, Fowler. Yes, the person probably walks away free," she said. "Of course, the appropriate jurisdiction has the option to retry the person in question."

"Thanks, Nancey, that information really helps." Beth thanked her as well and they agreed to get together at some point in the future.

Beth was grinning from ear to ear by the time we got to the car.

"That about ties it all together. It's the last piece of the puzzle. Why aren't you as happy about this as I am?" she asked with some concern.

"Nancey just confirmed what we already knew. But we're

not an inch closer to proving anything. The police won't act on what we know. No paper will print our suppositions. We can't prove squat. Even if we find the transcripts are missing, and we will, all we'll accomplish is to draw attention to ourselves. The authorities won't be able to tie the loss of the documents to the old man. You can bet he's covered those tracks well. We'll reap nothing but grief if we continue to dig. The men who killed the women are probably out of the country by now. If not, they're occupying a new dimension of existence. We keep on investigating and we might run into them in that new dimension. We will never prove a link between the murders and the Costillo family."

"What do you want to do? Should we go back to Nacogdoches and act as if nothing has happened? I can't tuck tail and run," she said as she scanned my face.

"We've got one trump left to play," I said. "We take what we have to K. Brad Turrow. He's not the type of man who'll allow this to work. I doubt if there's anything even Turrow can do to nail the old man for the hits, but he ought to be able to block the release of Paco. Turrow can do it without our being involved any further. . . . Beth, it makes sense. And it's the only course of action that does. If I thought we had a snowball's chance, I'd take the whole ride. But it's time to cut our losses."

She laid her head against the car door and some of the light had left her eyes. I hated being a part of this moment.

"Fowler, I promised you at the beginning that I'd do this your way. I'll keep my word. But I'm going to make you another promise right now. I don't know how or when, but I'll see these sons of bitches in hell before I'm through. I don't care if it takes the rest of my life." With that said, she got into the car. I suspect that Esteban Costillo felt a chill just then.

We drove back to the motel and tried to contact K. Brad Turrow. His secretary told me he was unavailable. I left an enticing message that suggested that I had new information concerning his son's family's murder. I left my home number.

Though it was a foregone conclusion in my mind, I con-

116

tacted the depositories of the official trial transcripts of the Costillo trial. In each case, the documents were missing. Since the agencies didn't communicate on the subject, none knew of the others' loss of the transcripts. The DA couldn't explain the missing tapes. They assured me that it was a clerical error and the tapes would be located. I didn't tell them not to bother.

Beth was sitting in a chair next to the window. She had been seemingly impervious to the conversation with Turrow's office. I took the other chair. She turned from the window and faced me.

"I remember the Christmas my parents gave me my first bike. It rained that morning and I couldn't ride it right away. I got mad at my parents. They were handy. You've given me a bike I can ride another day. I should be thanking you instead of causing you grief. . . . I'm sorry for the way I acted."

I repressed my urge to quote Eric Segal here. Levity probably wasn't the best response. Then there was also the risk of breaking new semantic ground in our relationship.

"No apology necessary. . . . If, however, you feel a little guilty, you could agree to leave your car here and drive back with me to Nacogdoches. You can use my car while you're there and I'll drive you back here whenever you wish."

I pulled her over to my lap. I encountered an amazingly hungry mouth. I took off her shirt and explored every inch of her upper body with my mouth. My normal passion was intensified by the energy generated by the frustration of the last couple of days. It was obvious that she was feeling the same way.

On the drive back we decided to alter the focus of her thesis. We would stay with the Wilson murder, but we would simply compare the various area coverages. It wouldn't be as exciting, but it would provide solid academic information. We agreed to meet Turrow together if a meeting took place at all.

As we approached town, Beth suggested that she move her things from the motel into my house. I was curious about the consequences of Anson trying to contact her. She told me that he was leaving the country for a few days.

"Minimal risk, maximum enjoyment," she said mischievously.

I had a couple of calls on the machine. The only one of consequence was from Case. He sounded antsy. I called him immediately and told him to come on over.

I had a feeling that Case was going to react negatively to what I had to say. Beth's presence might complicate the situation a little. I convinced her to take my car and go get her things.

The plug in Case's mouth was large enough to provide oral carcinoma for the entire redneck population of Angelina County.

I handed him his large soft-drink cup.

"How about a beer?" I asked.

Three beers and twenty minutes later Case was puckered to the max. I didn't think I'd ever seen him this speechless before. Eventually he ran his hand through his hair and sighed loudly.

"Shitfire, that's the goddamnest story I've ever heard," he said. "What the hell am I goin' to do now?"

"We can turn this into an asset as far as the election goes. Leave that to me. I'm going to take all this information to K. Brad Turrow. He's the only person I know who can do something with it," I said.

He got up and put on his hat. "This is going to chap my ass," he said.

"Yeah, I know. Won't do you any good to fret over it. We can't get the son of a bitch. Getting ourselves killed won't bring the Wilson woman back or salvage an ounce of justice. It'll just mean we're dead," I said.

He spit in the cup. He was real tight-jawed. "I ain't ever been any good at backin' off. I wouldn't like it to become habit formin'," he said with the intensity of a cornered cat. "Shit, Fowler, what ever happened to those days when right and wrong was real clear? I remember when there wasn't a hill too tall. What ever happened to those times?" he asked.

"Hell, Case, we grew up . . . and sometimes it's a real bitch," I answered.

Case hadn't been gone more than five minutes when Beth appeared. I told her about our conversation.

We prepared a gourmet dinner of popcorn and eggs. We stayed in for the evening, played some old music, and decided on the best approach to her thesis.

Next morning, Beth dropped me off at the college. She went to the offices of the *Lufkin Light, Tyler Herald,* and the *Nacogdoches Defender* to begin her research on their coverages of the investigation. As I sat at my desk and pondered the situation as it was taking form, it occurred to me that the witnesses in the original trial were probably fish bait by now. In the absence of the transcripts, should the DA attempt a retrial, their elimination would be essential to the scheme. I was toying with the idea of somehow warning the authorities about the witnesses when there came a knock at my office door.

Standing before me was Jimmy Wayne Ellis. He was wearing his usual shirt and tie.

"I'm sorry to bust in like this, Dr. McFarland. There wasn't anybody out there," he said, pointing to the outer office.

"Don't worry about it, Jim. Come in and close the door."

"Thanks. I need to talk."

"What's on your mind?" I asked.

"I gave a talk at the new prison about the program. They want me to come out three or four more times to help them set up a screening program for inmates who might someday be eligible for the PCR program."

"You got a problem with that?" I asked.

"One of the dates they want me there conflicts with our next meeting," he said.

"That's easy enough to rectify. We'll reschedule."

"Dr. McFarland, has the program got a chance of working?" he asked quietly.

"Tough question," I said. "Where's it coming from?"

"Shadows. In the shadows of my mind I wonder what's going to happen when one of the program's people back-

119

slides. I wonder if ten successful rehabilitations will balance out against one failure," he said thoughtfully.

"Should they?" I asked.

"Sometimes I'm sure they should. Other times I'm not so sure," he replied.

I wondered if Jimmy Wayne saw the old man and the boy during those times when he had doubts about the program.

"Is the program working for you?" I asked.

"I haven't done anything wrong in a long time. I feel like I'm helping people and setting an example. I know I want to live now," he said with a weak grin.

"Was there a time when you didn't?"

"For a while on the inside I wanted to die. In the joint lethal injection is called 'sweet death' when a man doesn't want to live any longer."

"You ever meet an inmate named Paco Costillo?" I asked.

"A stone killer. Some men kill out of anger. Some because they're out of control. Others in self-defense. Paco kills because he likes it. Most everyone is afraid of the boy because of his old man."

"Ever hear anything about K. Brad Turrow trying to kill Paco?" I asked.

"Some time back I heard somethin' about someone tryin' to kill the boy, but I don't know as I ever heard any mention of Mr. Turrow's name," he said. "Strange ain't it. . . . I mean . . . a man like Mr. Turrow . . . gets wronged like he was . . . and still tries to help people like me get on with life."

"I think we'd be on safe ground in saying that there aren't many men who would do what K. Brad Turrow is doing," I said sincerely.

"Dr. McFarland . . . it is possible for a man to rediscover his soul," he said as he left.

I was thinking about my conversation with Jimmy Wayne as I made my way to the faculty lounge. Cora and Hob were holding down the fort.

"What goes on?" I asked as I sorted through the mail, depositing most of it in the trash can near the Coke machine.

"We're talking about the woman skydiver over in the Carthage who was smushed yesterday when her chute didn't open," Cora said in a tone a mite too jovial for the subject.

"That sounds like a nasty way to go," I allowed.

"If it was me and my chute didn't open," Cora said, "I'd pull off my pants and spread my legs real far apart. That way, the wind resistance might slow my fall down some."

I was trying to get a view of that when Hob got up to leave. He looked at Cora and smiled.

"If my ex-wife had used that approach and jumped off our one-story house, it would've taken her three hours to hit the ground," he said with a pained look.

16

A Relationship Considered

It was nice and sunny and I was in need of a cold drink and warm companionship. I walked over to Tommy's to satisfy both wants. The place was very busy for an afternoon. Tommy was leaning on the bar looking like a Baptist who'd been caught having fun. I settled in next to him.

"A few more afternoons like this and you'll be able to pay the place off."

"Yeah," he said with something less than a gleeful tone in his voice. "I've got me a problem." He tossed the bar towel over his shoulder and looked at me with those big Irish eyes.

Was there something in the water? Why did everyone I meet need advice? And of all the people to turn to, why me? Most of the time I have trouble just getting me through the day.

"You'll keep in mind that free advice is usually overpriced," I said.

He looked around to make sure we weren't being overheard.

"Well, Fowler, the truth is that I've been keepin' time with a married woman for some time now." He spoke in his softest voice. "We've always been careful. Then, three nights ago her husband confronted her with suspicions about her seein' someone. He got a little violent. Nothin' major. Immature shit. He broke a table and kicked in a door. He grabbed her a couple of times and bruised her arm a bit." He stopped for a moment as a customer came near. I thought about how a real man is hard to find anymore. A really masculine table killer is even rarer to find. "He called her a lyin' bitch," he concluded with his voice sounding more mad than upset.

I sipped on my drink and quietly inventoried my priorities

of the moment. I had two murders, one insane Mafia patriarch, one affair of my own with a woman I didn't understand, a good friend on the verge of losing an election, and now a sentimental Irishman whose affair with a married woman had been discovered by her idiot husband. This was the stuff on which prime-time soaps were based.

"Why not stop seeing her. You not being in the picture has got to help stabilize the situation a little," I suggested, motioning for a refill.

"Fowler, I'm a mite more than just fond of the lady," Tommy mumbled with his head down.

"Tommy, get your shit together on this. In this state, up until a couple of years ago, they allowed wronged husbands to kill dumb Irish cocks like you. Even though the legislature repealed the paramour law, it's still a time-honored tradition in these parts. You keep on sneaking around this woman and you're liable to discover a couple of extra orifices in your body."

"I'll not be lettin' the asshole worry me," he said. I thought to myself how strange it is that drunks and lovers always feel bulletproof.

"There's something else too. If you're not going to make an honest woman of her, let her alone. If she's already got an asshole for a husband, she doesn't need another one for a lover," I argued.

"Does his reaction to his suspicions sound like that of a man who loves his wife?" he asked.

"Was he supposed to take the news in stride? Get a real hurt look on his face and ask his wife why she was seeing fit to sleep with another man? They would talk it over and discover the weaknesses in their relationship. After the talk he'd call you up and thank you for the therapeutic sex you had with his wife."

"Damn it, Fowler, I think . . . I know I love the woman. I think maybe she loves me too," he blurted more loudly than was his intent.

"Then have the girl get a divorce and marry her."

"We're both Catholic. Divorce is tough in our church," he explained while refilling my glass.

123

"Isn't it a little late to develop ulcers over Catholicism?" I asked with a little bite in my voice. "I mean, you've been involved in an immoral relationship for some time. As I recall the church has a fairly explicit policy with respect to infidelity. Why, all of a sudden, have your vows become so important?" I asked. Tommy's face screwed up something fierce. These were not the words he wanted to hear.

"Look, I'm not trying to be a prick. Sometimes I can't help it, I guess," I said with more empathy. "Tommy, your options seem clear to me. Either break it off and be good Catholics again—unhappy people if you love each other, but good Catholics—or get a divorce and get happily married. If the church is a problem, ignore it, rationalize it, or change churches. I'm an orthodox agnostic. I recommend it without equivocation." With that last bit of advice, I felt I had given him my best shot. I offered him a toast.

I walked back to the office and worked on college matters for a couple of hours. Beth was supposed to pick me up about six. She didn't call and wasn't there by six. I called Case and asked him to swing by and pick me up for the game.

Case wasn't overly conversational on the way to my house. He felt he needed to make an arrest or issue a statement about the investigation. Buck Meadows had been pressing the issue around town. I told him to hold off for another day while I waited for Turrow's call. I'd write an editorial for the local paper that would laud his refusal to play politics with the case. He could've, and a lesser man might've, arrested someone simply to look good in the election. He chose not to. He would end up looking pretty good for not trying to railroad Piligrew. I told him to issue a public statement implying that he was investigating a couple of pretty good leads that were too sensitive to be discussed in the papers and he'd come away looking real good in all of this. Case liked the sound of it. His attitude started to shift back to normal Case Bayhill.

"It just might work," he said with some enthusiasm.

I added to his new mood by pointing out that, aside from the murder, there wasn't a lot to bitch about in his administration. Crime was down. There were no cries of corruption or police harassment, and he was under budget.

"What does Buck bring to the office?" I asked. "He's a nice enough guy. Looks good in five-hundred-dollar Western suits. But he has no experience. He doesn't want to be chief of police. He wants to be governor. He's just using the office as a stepping stone. Folks around here know that."

He was clearly a new man. He went into the kitchen and found his Big Gulp cup. I made sure there was a new one in there every Tuesday night on the off chance he might actually hit the damn thing a couple of times. The group started showing up about seven or so. All the regulars were there. The primary subject of conversation was the murder. Case tried out his press release on the guys. It floated pretty well. Of course, they all felt they had a right to additional information concerning the sensitive leads. I was proud of Case. He sidestepped them as smoothly as shit through a goose.

I had some difficulty getting into the spirit of the game. It wasn't the guys. It was me. I was having trouble concentrating on the cards. I guess I just had too many things on my mind. Tim was the big winner, and I ended up losing about fifty dollars.

I turned off the lights and went into the living room. I opened the patio doors and sat on the floor against the fireplace. It was strangely quiet. Even the usual insect sounds were missing. Not a cricket or an owl could be heard. Occasionally, I heard the bug light's eulogy and then there was the constant rhythm of the ceiling fan. The moon was bright and the air still.

I've always had the ability to assign order in the midst of chaos. But no matter how hard I concentrated on the investigation, I kept lapsing back to Beth. My earlier conversation with Tommy kept coming back to me. Why was the nature of his relationship so clear to me and the nature of my own such a mystery? I wasn't sure what the next step ought to be. Beth was married and I didn't have a good feel for that relationship at all. Before long, she'd be through with her work in town. How would I handle her walking out of my life?

The opening of the front door interrupted my thoughts. Beth came into the room and deposited her papers on the coffee table.

"Now this is what I call soft lighting," she said.

"Deep thoughts are best pondered in deep darkness," I said from the shadows.

"I could use a cold drink and some of your moonlight," she said as she opened the refrigerator.

She came back to the living room and sat across from me with her back against the patio doorjamb. She looked good in the moonlight. Her hair rustled a little—a wisp of breeze had come up. She laid her head back against the door frame, closed her eyes, and let the day escape. She sipped on her drink for a minute, never opening her eyes. She pressed the cold drink against her cheek.

"Care to share some of those thoughts?" she asked softly.

"Lady . . . I've fallen in love with you. I'm not sure what to do about it," I said. She didn't say anything. She just sat there with her eyes closed. "I need to know where we stand."

"I don't know where we stand beyond right now," she said, opening her eyes and looking at the night sky. "I've always tried to be honest with myself and the people in my relationships. . . . We don't make any sense at all." There was a weak little smile on her face as she spoke. "There are a lot of things about me that you don't know. They make a difference in the way I have to deal with how I feel about you. . . . Am I making any sense at all?" she asked.

"I'm not going anywhere until you do," I answered.

"I'm not sure that I can give you any more than I've already given. I'm not sure that we can have any more than we've already had," she said, looking away again.

"Beth, right this minute I'm not real sure of a lot of things in my life. But there is one thing about which I'm absolutely sure. No one will ever love you any more or any better than I do right now. Regardless of what we decide to do about it, I'll survive. Lady, I can cope with the pain, but I want to know why," I said softly.

"I grew up too fast and I made a number of questionable

decisions. They were mine to make and I'll stand by them. Some people have moved through my life and left some scars. . . . Along came Anson and my life simplified. I'm good for him and he's good for me. . . . Then I came back here this summer. Being with you has clouded what was a pretty clear horizon. My life had some stability. I don't love him, but I like him. My mother told me once that you don't have to love a man to live with him. I grew to see the merit in her view. I was fully prepared to live my life in that context. Then I came back here this summer. I think I knew all along that you were too risky a variable. . . . But then, like a goddamn lemming I came back to the sea. . . . Fowler, I never buy on credit and I can't afford to love you," she said, looking me dead in the eyes.

A few years before, I had given a similar speech to a younger-than-her-years teenage girl right here in Nacogdoches. We'd dated steadily for a few months and even talked a little about marriage. All in the world that girl wanted was a husband, a house, and a family. I knew deep inside that I couldn't afford her dream. She would cost too much. After all, there were wrongs to be righted and glories to be won. She got married after I left for college. She eventually got that family.

Over the years, I've gone to sleep a few nights thinking about her. I guess what goes around comes around.

"I've never submitted totally to a man," she said as she came over and rested her head on my shoulder. "I've created the impression of submission, but I've never given my all. At this stage, I'm not sure that I'm capable of a love-based relationship. I'm afraid that going any further might ruin what we have. It may not be all we want it to be, but it's the most I've ever had."

Things were clearer and they were more vague. I thought of the line from an old song: "Did she get tired or did she just get lazy?"

"Fowler . . . I've had sex with several men. I've only made love with one. Make love to me again."

127

$\bigtriangledown$

17

K. Brad Turrow

THERE IS MORE THAN a little truth in the widely held notion that Texas millionaires tend to be rude, crude, and simpleminded. K. Brad was an exception to this rule. He was both articulate and bright. He had just enough Texas in his speech to do business in the oil patch. I sensed that he could turn it off and on at will.

The entire phone conversation took about three minutes. He was very efficient. We set up an appointment for lunch at one o'clock that afternoon. Turrow would fly in from Houston. At no time in the conversation had he mentioned the nature of our meeting.

Beth had rolled over a few seconds into the conversation and caught bits and pieces.

"There's not a way in this world that you're going to keep me from this meeting," she said with a look of a pissed Viking as she issued her ultimatum.

"The thought never crossed my cortical centers," I said with complete honesty. "I would like you to do a little pre-meeting digging, though. We need everything you can find on Turrow and the trial. See if you can add anything to what we already know."

"Where do you want to meet me?" she asked, getting out of the bed and starting for the bathroom.

"Drop me at the office on the way in and I'll see you back there at twelve-thirty," I replied.

We dressed quickly and by ten I was at the office and Beth was at the library.

The remainder of my morning was occupied with relatively mundane school business. Time passes awfully slowly when you're anxious.

Beth showed up a few minutes early. "It was pretty much as we were told," she said. "The evidence against Paco was irrefutable. They had a fiber match from the son's sweater found in the van. A fingerprint found in the van matched the prints of the hooker. Turrow's reward lured a couple of people out of the woodwork. They provided some solid corroborative evidence. One interesting note: While in jail awaiting trial, one of the bodyguards was found with his throat cut and his tongue missing. The DA was quoted as saying that the nature of the killing was a warning to those who might be tempted by the Turrow rewards. It's my guess that the Costillo people somehow got to the judge. This should've been a death penalty situation," she concluded.

"What's your impression of Turrow?" I asked.

"He makes a good friend and a very bad enemy. He kicks ass and takes names," she said.

We decided on the restaurant in the Holiday Inn for the lunch meeting. In small Texas towns there are two constants with respect to places to eat—the Dairy Queen and the Holiday Inn. It was also very near the small local airport where Turrow's private plane would arrive.

We were seated at a table for eight in the most secluded part of the room. I told the waitress we were expecting another party shortly. I gave her my name and we ordered something to drink. The girl had just left when I caught sight of a man making his way to our table. He was tastefully dressed in a dark blue suit that had never seen a rack. He looked to be about sixty years old and was starting to show his years. His gray hair, cut short, and his sun-dried skin were testament to his having weathered a few years. He stood about six feet tall and had what must once have been a sturdy build. His gait was that of a successful man.

He extended his hand. If he was surprised to see Beth, he didn't show it. I introduced her as a colleague. He spoke with ease and purpose at the same time. He looked you in the eye when he talked to you. I liked him instinctively; he was approachable and real.

Seated not too far away were two sets of men. They occupied two tables on either side of the entrance. They were all wearing suits that couldn't be found in Nacogdoches. Otherwise they were really pretty good at blending in.

He motioned for the waitress and ordered a chicken-fried steak and a cold beer. With the exception of the beer, we ordered the same.

"Fowler, I should tell you that I'm an old fan of yours. I really enjoyed your book, and I'm very pleased that you decided to join the rehabilitation project. Any chance it has of success rests in efforts of concerned people like yourself." He spoke with the tone of a man not given to bullshit diplomacy.

"Thank you," I said as I tried to get a firm fix on the man. "And I must say that I've always been amazed and impressed by your sponsorship of the project, given your tragedy."

"It was an ordeal that taught me a great deal about our system of justice. Our prison system is overcrowded and, consequently, it's inevitable that some of our worst offenders will be released. It's commonsensical to develop programs to optimize the possibility of successful reintegration," he said with ease.

He turned his attention to Beth.

"I've always considered journalism an interesting and important business," he said. "I've owned a couple of newspapers and found them to be fascinating."

"Lately, it's really picked up in intensity," she said.

Turrow was a blend of Eastern schools and Southwestern upbringing. He exuded competence. "Your message implied that you had some information concerning the murder of my son and his family," he said.

I toyed with my steak and filled him in on the details of our investigation. He listened intently and offered no comment. He seemed uninterested in his food as well. Beth, on the other hand, assaulted her steak like a relief victim.

When I had finished my story, he ordered another beer and excused himself from the table for a minute. As he

130

headed in the direction of the men's room, he was joined by one of his people.

"What do you think?" she asked me quietly.

"About what?" I replied.

"About Turrow, about what you think he's going to do now that he knows everything," she said.

"You only get what he wants you to get. I'm not sure he knows what he's going to do, just yet."

He was back at the table in less than five minutes. His first action was to take a blue-collar chug on his beer.

"What you've told me is alarming for several reasons, not the least of which is that people have been killed. But I'm curious as to why you've come to me as opposed to the Houston police." He seemed to be carefully measuring every word.

"A close friend of mine is now the regional director for the FBI in the Houston area. We discussed the situation at length and decided against going to the police. The Costillo organization has too many ears in the department. And if we're right about all of this, how could they afford to let us live to continue digging?"

"Sound reasoning. From what I know about Esteban, you're at risk if he even suspects that you pose a threat to his plans. However, that still leaves me wondering why you decided to bring the information to me," he said.

"Pretty simple really," I said, looking him straight in the eyes. "You represent the best shot at thwarting Costillo's plan without our getting killed in the process. You have more reason than anyone else I know of to see to it that Paco stays in prison. In addition to which, you also have sufficient resources on all levels to get the job done right. From what we've been able to find out, you'll do these things with discretion."

I continued. "I don't see any way for the customary legal channels to secure any reasonable measure of justice here. It seems to me to require expertise in arenas not accessible to Beth and me. A matter more suited to politicos than old cops and fledgling reporters."

He leaned back and finished his beer slowly.

"Again, tough to fault your reasoning. You're dealing with animals, not humans," he said. His eyes had suddenly gone cold. It was the first and last time we'd see anything resembling emotion in the man. It was just a flash, but it was enough to get my hopes up. I was sure that K. Brad Turrow was about to extend the full power of his billion-dollar empire to our common cause. I was wrong, about as wrong as a man can be.

"I'll see to it that the appropriate people are informed of your theory," he said as he regained his dispassionate demeanor once again. "Of course, I'll see to it that your names are kept out of it entirely."

The heavy silence compelled him to further explain his timid decision. For the first time since he sat down, he chose to avoid our eyes in favor of his empty glass. "When my boy and his family were murdered, I did everything in my power to bring those responsible to justice. I believe in this country and its institutions. My wife and I invested our very blood in the investigation and the months of trial. Invested too much. . . . Two days after the verdict, Wanda suffered a severe stroke. She's still hospitalized. Hell, my doctors tell me that my own heart is hanging on by the proverbial thread. Any more stress, I'm told, will kill me."

This was not the man I had read about, not the man Greenburg had spoken of. This was but a shell of that man. He pushed his untouched food aside and got up to leave.

"Folks," he said, looking at both of us, "these creatures are dangerous beyond most people's comprehension. Leave this here. Drop it and walk away while you can . . . don't look back. Let the higher powers take care of this as best they can."

With that, he left with his silent entourage.

Beth watched his every step as he made his way out. She watched the door close after them. We didn't talk for a few seconds.

"I don't think I've ever misjudged anyone as badly as I did one K. Brad Turrow," she said, shifting her focus back to me.

"What happened to his grit? All the life's been sucked out of the man. I don't think he's going to do a damned thing. And that means the slimy bastards will get away with it," she said through gritted teeth.

A little voice was telling me that something wasn't right here, but it was that same little voice that told me to bet a hundred dollars on the University of Houston to win the NCAA tournament against North Carolina State a few years back. I wrote off the hundred dollars as tuition. I guess I'd known all along that I had no right to expect more from someone else than I was willing to do myself. It was clear to me now that I wasn't going to be able to simply walk away from this clean.

The milk gravy was paste and the steak had the appeal of cardboard. We decided to go back to my house and cuss and plan.

Beth made a beeline for the bar, poured a stiff Scotch, and dropped a large floor pillow near the hearth. "So, what's up, doc?" she asked without enthusiasm. She'd left most of her starch in the restaurant.

"There's the possibility that K. Brad will get the information to the right people and they'll at least scuttle the effort to get Paco out. . . . There's even a remote possibility that K. Brad will grow some balls and do some serious ass-kicking himself," I said, unable to generate much enthusiasm.

The last possibility bought a sarcastic look from Beth. I switched on the answering machine to hear Kermit's distinctive voice.

"Fowler, it's imperative that we meet tonight. Don't try to call me. Meet me at Dirty's at six this evening."

"That's interesting," Beth said as she made an attempt to sit up. "What do you make of it?"

"I'm not sure. Greenburg's not given to melodramatics. The man doesn't spook easily. It's got to have something to do with his digging for us in the Costillo thing."

"We'll have to get on the stick if we're going to get there by six," she said, looking at the clock.

"You're not going," I said firmly. "I don't know what he's found, but you've got to be safer here than in Houston."

I could see the protest in her eyes.

"Don't even try. I'm going alone."

She agreed to stay in Nacogdoches. I called Case and had a black-and-white maintain high visibility around the house.

I didn't want to leave Beth afoot, so I decided to get a school vehicle for the trip.

18

A Good Friend Dies

I USED THE DRIVE to Houston to mull over the investigation. Turrow's reaction was all wrong. His eyes weren't the eyes of a beaten man. His whole life was a contradiction to his reactions at the meeting. Why come all the way to Nacogdoches if you weren't prepared to invest more in the situation? A little voice was telling me that there was too much inconsistency here. Was K. Brad blowing a little smoke up my ass? If so, why?

In my preoccupation with thinking about the investigation I had forgotten about the damned Houston freeway system. It took me two hours to drive the first one hundred and twenty miles and almost that long to drive the last twenty. Janis Joplin was telling me all about Bobby McGee when I parked in the lot at Dirty's a couple of minutes past six. I've never understood how she got the last line of that song on the radio.

The place was a fairly typical west Houston novelty bar and eatery. Happy hour and buffalo wings were the order of the day. It was crowded and loud. I looked around for Kermit and didn't see him anywhere. I asked one of the two bartenders if he knew Kermit Greenburg. The guy's name was Alex. He told me he not only knew Greenburg but that he had called a few minutes before I came in and asked him to tell someone named Fowler to wait at the bar. I headed for the men's room. About halfway back to the bar, I saw Kermit come in the front door. He didn't see me. He walked to the bar and spoke to Alex. A guy sitting there nursing a drink said something to him and Kermit turned in his direction.

At that precise moment I heard the sound of gunshots.

I'd been around weapons long enough to recognize the explosions of high-caliber weapons. The place became chaotic. People were screaming and diving under tables and onto the floor. I caught a glimpse of Kermit reeling into the bar. The man he had turned toward took a head shot. His forehead exploded like a ripe melon and blood and brain tissue went everywhere. The bartender was hit in the arm. In the confusion, it was hard to get a clear view of the shooters. There were two of them and they were Hispanic. Kermit never had a chance. There were nearly a dozen shots fired. He never pulled his gun. They turned and casually walked from the room. I heard a couple of additional shots outside. I later found out they had encountered an unlucky off-duty, uniformed police officer as they exited. He never knew what hit him.

I wasn't sure how many times Kermit had been shot. I saw his body react several times on its way to the floor. When I got to him, he was lying facedown in a pool of blood. The guy who had been next to him was spread-eagled on the bar. A good portion of his head was now decor. Liquor bottles were shattered and dripping. The area looked like a war zone.

I bent down and rolled Kermit over as gently as I could. He wasn't dead, but wasn't far from it. He was shot to hell. He had wounds in the left shoulder, the neck, and the back. A part of his left ear had been blown away. I heard someone calling for an ambulance. It would never do Kermit any good. Aside from any internal injuries, his blood loss was already fatal. He opened his eyes. His breathing was labored and sporadic. He was trying to speak. This was one tough son of a bitch. By all rights he should've been dead. But he'd made up his mind to stay alive until he'd told me something. He was having trouble holding enough air to speak. His voice was raspy and soft. He pulled my face to his mouth. It was all I could do to make out a few whispers.

"Gutterman . . . Stephen Gutterman . . ." His voice trailed off and I thought I'd heard his last words. The veins in his neck were straining as he tried to finish. "Costillo knows . . . killed me . . . careful . . . he knows . . . lemure . . . lemure." He stopped breathing at the same time he stopped talking. I sat there with the head of my good friend in my lap. In a few minutes, the police, the medics, and the press would arrive. Tonight there would be a story about another bar shooting in Houston on the late news and tomorrow night some guy would be hustling a secretary on this very spot.

I didn't know the homicide detective who was in charge. His name was James Chance. He looked a little young to be a crime-scene control officer, but he handled everything very professionally.

The witnesses to the shooting numbered about a hundred. We were divided up into five groups and placed as far apart in the building as possible. Each group was being questioned by a two-man team. The forensics people wee busily going about their tasks. Chance was overseeing every detail and dropping in and out of each of the witness groups. I kept falling further and further back in the group. I used the time to get my thoughts together about what I was going to tell them. If I'd understood Kermit's closing words correctly, the old man now knew about us. In which case, we probably had nothing to lose if I told the cops everything I knew.

It wasn't long before Detective Chance paid me a visit. He'd discovered from Alex that Kermit was there to meet with me. By this time they knew that he had been an FBI agent. That fact would complicate the investigation for HPD. There would be the inevitable jurisdictional problems between the federal and local agencies. The death of an agent would bring in the Feds like locusts. On the other hand, nothing, but nothing, was as enjoyable for a local cop as solving a major case ahead of the bureau. It didn't happen often, but when it did, careers were made at the local level and impaired at the federal level.

I had dried blood all over my clothes. He asked if I'd been injured at all, then told me that we would talk about all of this at the central police station a little later on. Detective Joel Ashford was assigned to escort me.

Not questioning me at the scene was a smooth move.

Taking me to the downtown station was another slick maneuver. It was policy in Houston to take witnesses and mobile victims to the nearest police substation for interrogation. By getting me away from the scene, he kept me away from the FBI for a while. If the Feds found out about me, hiding me somewhere other than the local substation would buy him some additional time. He knew I was hot and he put me in the best possible position to help the HPD solve the case.

I got to the station a few minutes before Chance arrived there. I used the time to clean up a little and convinced Ashford to let me call Beth. I explained the situation and told her to call Case and have a black-and-white stay the night in the driveway. I told her I'd try to make it home that night. Ashford left me alone for a minute, so I got in touch with Allusoto. He told me he'd be at the station in fifteen minutes.

Detective Chance entered the station with a couple of the cops from the crime scene. I was waiting in a glass-enclosed office with a view of the main room. Before he could get to me, he was waylaid by two men who looked important. They got his undivided attention. His distraction gave me a little more time to think about the evening. The more I thought about the hit, the more I was convinced that the Costillo family was on to us. A pro never makes a hit in a crowded place unless it's his only option. There are too many people to get in the way. There are too many witnesses. In this case, the parking lot was made to order for the hit. If he had gotten inside before they could get it done, then they would normally have simply waited for him to leave and gotten him on the way out. There was only one explanation that made any sense of the Hollywood-style shoot-out in the bar. The hitters were assuming that he was meeting someone there. Their instructions were to take both people out. I ran the shooting through my mind again. When Kermit came in he didn't see me. He stopped at the bar and then turned to say something to the fellow sitting next to where he was standing. It was when he turned to say something to that guy that the shooting started. The hitters must have thought they'd killed us both. Maybe they'd figure me dead now. Telling Chance everything might elevate me to target status again. I heard Allusoto as he entered the outer office. He got involved in the conversation with Chance and the other two. Eventually they headed toward the office where I was waiting. Danny didn't look any too happy.

The little office was crowded with the five of us. It turned out that the other two men were the chief assistant district attorney and the station captain. Even with the wigs in the room, Chance was in charge of the interrogation. The others were observers. Their presence meant that the case was special. Their silence meant that they considered Chance special as well. For his part, Detective Chance had an aura of control about him. He had a thirty-year-old body and a fifty-year-old face. He was dressed fashionably. He looked more like a downtown lawyer than a detective.

"Mr. McFarland," he said in a deep, soft voice, "why were you at the bar this evening?"

I told him that I'd had an appointment with Greenburg for around six o'clock.

"What was to be the nature of this meeting?" he asked as he checked the tape recorder to make sure it was functioning properly. He then pulled a plastic bag from his coat and extracted a toothpick. He put it between his teeth and played with it. Why did all of these guys have an oral fixation? It was always cigarettes, pipes, or toothpicks. I wondered if that meant they had or hadn't been bottle babies.

I told them of my investigation into the Wilson murder. I omitted Beth. I justified my curiosity in the matter as relating to my friendship with the Nacogdoches chief of police and, to a lesser extent, my past association with the FBI. I filled them in on the possible connection between the Wilson murder and the Vanhorbeck killing. I made a snap decision to tell them about the possible connection of the Costillo family to both killings. The mention of the name got an immediate reaction from everyone in the room. I didn't tell them about my meetings with Allusoto and Turrow.

"So you believe Agent Greenburg asked you to meet him to tell you something about the murders?" he asked, rolling the toothpick around in his mouth.

"That would be my best guess," I replied.

"It's my understanding that Agent Greenburg said something to you before he died. Exactly what did he say?" he asked firmly.

The assistant DA's mouth was open and his eyes were wide. This was the type of case that made detectives into captains and assistant DAs into grown-ups.

I told them what he said save for "lemure." I wasn't sure what he'd said anyway. Instinctively I withheld that word. I'm not real sure why.

Chance had moved on to a second toothpick. I wondered if the importance of the case could be measured by the number of toothpicks he went through. You could see the wheels turning in the room as Greenburg's mumblings were being decoded by all present.

"What was the connection you and the agent saw between the Costillo family and the two murders?" He removed the latest wood sliver from his mouth and wiped the moisture off his upper lip with his hand.

I explained what I thought the connection to be. Chance was intrigued by the reasoning. Like myself, he knew that all the small clues added up to but one conclusion. It all made sense to him as well. I could see it in his eyes.

"Why didn't you contact the local police with your suspicion?" he asked. The room atmosphere got a little heavy. Allusoto's asshole puckered so much I thought the chair cushion would disappear from view. I was sure that he was airtight.

"The thought crossed my mind, but I didn't have any hard evidence. I played the whole story for the police in Nacogdoches and got laughed at. I've known and worked with Detective Allusoto for years. If I'd have come up with anything substantial, I'd have contacted him. After talking to Greenburg the first time, I'd about decided to put the whole thing to bed and leave it." I paused and looked directly at Chance.

"You know how it is when you know something in your gut, but you can't prove it."

He once again flashed that little, almost imperceptible smile. If he was as smart as I was giving him credit as being, he had that gut feeling right now.

"Tell us your version of the events that transpired at the restaurant earlier this evening," he asked.

I described the situation as clearly as possible. I avoided speculations about my being a target.

"Mr. McFarland, I appreciate your cooperation in all of this. I'm sure that there'll be other questions, possibly from other police organizations. I realize that you probably need to go back to Nacogdoches, but please keep a couple of things in mind. This case has some very ominous overtones to it. If your theory is correct, it's possible that you were supposed to have been killed this evening. Assuming that you've told us everything you know, it's also possible that you're no longer a target. Silencing you wouldn't be important any longer. There are no guarantees of that, however." Chance got up and left with the two men with whom he entered.

"How straight were you with him?" Danny asked without moving from his original seat.

"Everything I told him was the truth," I said, knowing that he understood the limitations of that statement.

"Look, Fowler," he offered, "they're going to run with what you gave them. This is a potential career builder. The only thing that'll slow 'em down is tripping over their tongues. . . . We both know they're pissin' into a strong wind. They ain't going to get Costillo on this. If we got lucky and tied someone in his organization into it, the son of a bitch would become organic fertilizer in a matter of minutes," he said as he got up and threw away his plastic coffee cup. We left the building without any additional conversation on the subject. He asked if I wanted to stay the night at his place or at least go over and clean up. I told him that all I wanted to do was to get back to Nacogdoches as soon as possible.

Danny talked incessantly as he drove me back to my car. It was still parked in the lot at Dirty's.

141

"If we were dealing with any other crime family I know of, you wouldn't have much to worry about now that we know of the plan. But these crazy motherfuckers aren't your everyday Mafia family. They're unprofessional and unpredictable. The goddamn dope business is just plain ruining crime. They may decide to kill you for the hell of it. You need to disappear for a while," he said with disgust in his voice.

"Pull into that Sonic will you?" I asked, ignoring, for the moment, his last remark. "All of a sudden I'm a little hungry. . . . I can't bring myself to run from these people any more than I already have. I don't have the time or the inclination. These lice have killed an entire family, a schoolteacher, a court reporter, a hooker, an off-duty cop, an innocent bystander, and a good friend. I might be able to hide from them, but I couldn't hide from myself. I've got to do something. I just don't know what yet."

The carhop took my order and tried to survive the mosquito attack on her way back to the grill.

"By the way, in case I forget to tell you later, thanks for your covering my ass about our earlier meeting on this. If they ever found out that I was remotely aware of any of this before the shooting, I'd be chin-deep in sheepshit," he said, stumbling through a difficult communication. I ignored his comment altogether.

While I wolfed down the burger, Danny went to the trunk and came back with something wrapped in a towel. It was a nine-millimeter Browning automatic. There were two clips with it.

"This piece is as cold as an ex-wife's smile. It's not traceable," he assured me as he slid the clip into the handle and primed the chamber.

It had been a long time since I'd carried a gun. I'd never liked them. I didn't even own one any longer.

"Fifteen shots . . . semiautomatic . . . no jam . . . aim and shoot," he said as he went through he motions.

"I vaguely remember how to use one of these," I said with a grin.

"Look, buddy," he said seriously, "you can't hesitate with

142

these people. Right now you got to get your mind out of the college classroom and back on the streets. If you don't get some edge back, you're going to die."

In two minutes we were back at Dirty's and I was standing next to my car.

"Danny, thanks for the gun."

"What fuckin' gun is that," he said as he drove off.

I put the gun on the seat next to me and headed for home. For two hours I thought about Kermit Greenburg.

19

The Bureau Comes Through

T HE BIG CLOCK ON the First Republic Bank of Nacogdoches flashed 2:15. Temperature a cool 77 degrees. I was dead tired but only a couple of blocks from Beth. I pulled up to a red light. Next to me was a Volkswagon convertible with the top down. In it were four kids with the radio on too loud. I recognized "My Girl" by the Temptations. They were laughing and having a good time. I wondered if any of them understood what a perfect night this really was. There's no way to explain the feeling of being young and in lust on a clear cool night with just the right music playing too loud. I remembered a night like it in the summer of 1969. I had thirty-five dollars and my dad's new LTD. I was on my way to see the legendary "Juicy" Luci Johnston. As I recalled, the song at the red light that night was "Knock Three Times." I remembered looking around and thinking to myself that it couldn't get any better than this. I was right.

The light changed and the Volkswagon cruised off toward the countryside. I envied those kids their temporary ambivalence to all things significant. I couldn't resist. I left a little rubber and wondered if Luci was still juicy. I hoped so. The black-and-white was in the driveway. Dewey was asleep at the wheel. I didn't wake him.

All was quiet. The only noise was the buzzing of the bug light. I had long believed that the person who invented the device was more an expert on human nature than a serious insect engineer. Every house in Texas probably had at least one. Poot Potter had twelve of them strategically located around his house. The constant noise generated by a dozen of the things has been the source of several complaints to the police. The damned things can't possibly electrocute enough bugs to make a serious impact on the area's mosquito population. On the other hand, they're worth the cost just to hear the sound of another of the little bastards getting fried alive. I know it makes me feel real good.

Beth was waiting at the door. In spite of my efforts to clean up at the station, there were still bloodstains on everything I was wearing. She didn't say anything. She just stood there and looked at me. A couple of tears began to trickle down her cheeks. She met me halfway up the walk and hugged me. I could feel the relief in her arms.

After a shower I lay down with my head in her lap. I started to tell her of the night's events. She stroked my hair and told me it could wait until morning. I didn't argue. The last thing I remembered was the feel of Beth's fingers.

I slept hard for about five hours. But I found myself wide-awake and sitting there looking at Beth as she continued to sleep. She looked so vulnerable lying there. She shifted positions a little and her foot touched mine. It was ice-cold. Her feet were always cold. How could such a radioactive body have perpetually cold feet? I was pondering that question when I noticed her looking at me. "Good morning, lady," I said as I reached for a lock of her hair.

"And a good mornin' to you," she said with a raspy, sleepy voice. I pulled her up into my arms for a little early morning snuggling.

"Want to tell me about last night?" she asked quietly.

I started from the beginning and filled her in on every detail.

"It looks to me as if we've been made by the bad guys," she said matter-of-factly. "I guess there is an upside in that we don't have to be so concerned about them finding out about us anymore."

"Does the name Stephen Gutterman mean anything to you?" I asked.

"No," she replied. "What do you make of that last word? How do you spell it?"

"I don't know what to make of it. It doesn't mean anything

to me. Sounded foreign. I don't know, maybe *l-e-m-u-r-e*," I answered.

She got up and pulled a dictionary from the bookcase in the study.

"There's a lemur. That's a small animal with large eyes. Then there's lemures. In ancient Rome, lemures were the name given to evil spirits. I don't see an obvious application of the term to what we're working on," she said, shaking her head.

"Hell . . . I'm probably not spelling the word properly. Right this minute, it's not that important to me. What is important is you. The shooting has convinced me that you're in too much danger," I said as I found the floor with my feet.

Her response was immediate. She cocked her head to one side and flashed me a look of disbelief.

"What the hell do you mean?" she growled. Her eyes started to narrow and her jaw started to set. "Look, Fowler, if you're going to lapse into another of your periods of chauvinistic protection bullshit, I'll save Costillo the trouble of killing you. I'll do it myself right now," she said firmly. "I can take care of myself, goddamn it. I'm in this for the duration, remember? Don't even think about shuttling me off somewhere until the menfolk feel it's safe."

"Kermit's murder raises the ante significantly," I said, putting on my pants. "When you kill an FBI agent in a crowded bar, it means that there are no limits to what you'll do. I really think they were looking for me in that bar as well. And if they're as connected as I think they are, it won't be long before they find out they missed me. When that happens, I think they'll make another trip to Nacogdoches."

"Maybe so, but where would I go that they couldn't find me?" she asked. "I've got a husband in Houston that they'll find out about. Come on, stop thinking with your heart. If we've got any chance at all, it lies in finding out the whole story and going public. Give the cops hard proof and break the story statewide. Then even old Esteban might find it a little risky coming after us."

146

Everything she was saying made sense. Even people hidden in the witness program got discovered and killed. Anson would always be there to be used to leverage her out of hiding. How long would she have to hide, anyway? Our best chance did rest in putting so much heat on Costillo that he couldn't afford to take us out.

"You're too hardheaded for your own good, you know?" I said. "I don't think your parents spanked you near enough when you were young."

"But I'm right and you know it," she said. "Come on, admit it, I'm right."

"Let's just say that there is some merit in what you say," I replied. "When a man fights for life for only one reason, then the reason has to be pretty important. If we can find out about Gutterman and 'lemure' we might just have the type of information we need." I paused to get a drink. "Danny gave me a gun. I think it would be a good idea if we carried it with us."

"What kind of gun?" she asked.

"It's a Browning automatic," I replied.

"Fifteen shots, safety on the right side?" she asked as she contemplated some toast. I don't know why, but it never occurred to me that she would know anything about guns.

"That's right," I said, sounding surprised.

"Don't sound so shocked," she said, having decided to forgo the toast. "I grew up around guns of all types. My father owned a few rentals. Occasionally a renter would get in arrears and my dad would always take guns instead of cash. I can load them, shoot them, and clean them," she said with confidence.

"That's good to know. Do you bait hooks and clean fish too?" I asked with a smile.

The phone rang. It was Case. He was pissed to the max. He did interrupt his tirade to tell me he was glad that I was all right. It was, however, only a brief respite. He quickly got back into the torrent of complaints. Number one on his list was the fact that I hadn't contacted him last night. Number two was the fact that a team of FBI agents were going to be

147

in his office in an hour to question me. He had about a dozen predictable questions, which he fired in rapid succession. When he finally paused for breath, I jumped in and told him I'd be in his office in half an hour. I promised to clear up this whole thing.

Dewey pulled out behind us as we backed out of the drive. On the way to the station Beth inspected the gun. She handled it with ease and expertise. I was impressed.

We walked into the police station on time to the minute. Case's secretary, Annie, ushered us right into his office. He was sitting at his desk, deeply immersed in something. He was chewing an enormous plug.

"Annie"—he spit and continued—"when the federal boys get here don't tell 'em Fowler's here. Feed 'em, give 'em some coffee, flirt, tell jokes, strip—hell, do whatever it takes to keep 'em occupied till I'm ready for 'em. That clear?" he asked.

Annie Marsh had worked for Case far too long to get caught up in his frequent panics. She nodded and made her way for the door.

"It's a cryin' goddamn shame about Greenburg," he said after releasing another twenty or so ounces of liquid cancer. "Hell of a cop and a good guy. What's it all about? I got this terrible feelin' in the pit of my stomach that you and sweet-cakes are about to go snorkelin' in a big septic tank somewhere."

It took ten minutes to fill him in on all of it because he kept interrupting me with questions.

"You figure these Mexes will try to take you out up here?" he asked.

"That's a possibility . . . a real possibility," I said.

"How do you want to play this with the Feds?" he asked.

"I guess we'll just have to play it by ear."

"I'll cover as much of your ass as I can," he said, smiling at Beth.

"One last thing," I said. "We're going after these people. I don't know how we're going to do it yet, but we're going to see to it that Paco never sees the light of a free day."

148

He didn't say a word. He just looked at me with those steel-blue eyes and chewed thoughtfully.

"Come on, Wensel Orley, show some balls," I said.

He walked over to the wastepaper basket and emptied his mouth. "Oh, I'll show you some balls all right. I just hope they ain't in my hand at the time."

Annie stuck her head in the door and told us that the guests had arrived and she had put them in the conference room with a pot of coffee and a box of donuts.

"I guess it's time to shit or get off the pot," he said. "Let's see what's on Uncle Sam's mind."

I told him that I wanted Beth in the room, but I didn't want them to know of her involvement unless it became necessary. He picked up a legal pad and a pencil. He handed them to Beth as he went by.

"Sweetcakes, you've been promoted from reporter to secretary. Try to show some appreciation for the increase in status. And try to look like you know what you're doin', will ya?" he asked.

Beth smiled her tolerant smile. The conference room was where the city council met. It was the nicest room in the courthouse. It had fake leather chairs, air-conditioning, and a large solid-wood conference table. Along the walls were portraits of the past governors of Texas. They were all there, save for the previous governor, Mark White. In his place was a picture of the 1984 Nacogdoches High School football team, all nine of the academically eligible players.

Seated at the conference table were two men with open briefcases. They introduced themselves as agents Georgis and Corder. Agent Corder was thirty or so, with the look of a man who could take care of himself. He looked to be fit and women would probably find him handsome in an outdoorsy sort of way. Thomas Georgis, the older of the two, appeared to be in charge. He was a tall, friendly-looking man with gray hair, sad eyes, and the strangest nose I'd ever seen. It was long and narrow, but bulbous and crimson-red on the end. It looked as though a hornet had stung him flush on the nose. I initially assumed that to be the case; however,

149

upon further, but discreet, observation, I concluded that this was a naturally ugly nose. Georgis wore a brown Brooks Brothers suit and Corder wore the blue version of the same suit. Given the nose, I thought Georgis would've coordinated better with the blue one.

Case handled the introductions for our side.

"Dr. McFarland, it's a pleasure to meet you," Agent Georgis said as he extended his hand. "My old supervisor, Asa Dureen, spoke very highly of you. He considered you to be one of the really outstanding agents in the bureau. He took your decision to leave pretty hard. Said the bureau couldn't stand the loss of people like you."

I had worked with Asa Dureen my first three years with the bureau. He was a tough-as-nails old-liner who took the job seriously. I valued his opinion.

"Asa's gotten old and his memory isn't what it used to be," I said after shaking hands with both of them.

"As you know, the death of an agent involves an investigation of extraordinary proportions. Agent Greenburg was supervising some extremely important matters for the bureau and his loss is particularly difficult to deal with. I mean no disrespect, but we're going to have to do this by the book," he said as he placed a tape recorder in front of me.

It's always awkward dealing with an ex-agent. There's the question of how much respect to show the person. Good agents learn that nothing can be allowed to interfere with the investigation. Ex-agents worth respect know that.

"Wouldn't have it any other way," I said evenly.

Georgis explained my rights.

"What was the nature of your relationship with Kermit Greenburg?"

While Georgis asked the questions, Corder kept a close eye on my every move. They were pretty good. Asa would be pleased.

"I considered him a good friend. I met him in 1974. He came to the Houston office just as I was made the regional supervisor. He worked under my supervision for several years."

150

"So when the professional relationship ended, you continued to have a personal relationship with him. Would that be a correct assessment of the situation?" he asked.

"Yes."

"The bartender at the club where the shooting occurred has stated that Agent Greenburg told him to be on the lookout for you that night. He further stated that you asked him personally if Agent Greenburg was there. Are these statements correct?"

"Yes."

"So the night of Agent Greenburg's murder, the two of you were planning to meet at the club called Dirty's. Is that correct?"

"Yes."

"What was the purpose of that meeting, Dr. McFarland?" he asked.

"I'm not sure. He was killed before we had an opportunity to talk," I said, choosing my words carefully.

The agents subtly glanced at each other. That was not the answer they expected. Case looked a little tense. Beth's eyes were transfixed on Georgis's nose. I was having some trouble avoiding it myself.

"Even though you didn't get the opportunity to consummate the meeting, surely you have an idea of the reason for it," he said in a slightly accusatory tone.

"I received a message on my recorder that said it was imperative that I meet him at Dirty's by six P.M. on the day in question. Any thoughts about his reason for wanting me to be there would be speculation at best," I responded.

Georgis's face flushed the color of his nose. Corder's expression remained unchanged.

"For a good friend, you don't seem overly eager to help us catch the people responsible for Kermit Greenburg's murder," he said with obvious restraint.

I liked both his reaction and his efforts to control it. The flashes of anger showed he cared and the control showed that he was a professional.

I reached over and switched off the recorder.

"Just so we're all on the same page here. No one in this room wants the bastards who killed Kermit more than I do. But the sad fact is . . . he's dead . . . and for the moment, at least, I'm alive. You boys are too smart not to have some sense of what this is all about. I think it's in my best interest to work with you on this, but you've got to work with me at the same time." My voice left little room for argument.

Georgis looked at Corder for a few seconds. Leaving the recorder off meant that they were willing to see where I was going at least.

"It's clear to me that the Costillo family killed Kermit and tried to kill me at the same time. One of the victims at the scene was an innocent bystander whom they mistook for me."

"With all due respect, Dr. McFarland, upon what do you base that supposition?" Georgis asked.

"I'm coming to that," I said, preparing to play my trump card. "I know everything you need to know about the case that Kermit and I were working on. I think that case was the reason he was killed. I'll give you everything I have on the condition that you give me everything you have that's related."

"I don't think we can do that," Georgis said quickly. "Besides, you above anyone else should know that you're not in a bargaining position. Legally, we can force you to tell us what you know about the crime."

"Maybe, but you know that my ass is on the line here. I need a trump card. Information is that trump. I have a number of pieces to the puzzle, but there are a few missing. Where my life is concerned, I'd just as soon be on top of the situation," I said firmly.

"You are aware that we have an excellent witness protection program?" Corder pointed out.

"Spare me the standard line," I said, cutting him off from any further elaboration on the program. "In the first place, my life wouldn't be worth a plugged nickel in the damn program. The people we're dealing with can buy the program and everyone in it. We all know that. The days when the program was secure are long gone. In the second place, I'm not running or hiding from these lice. You ready to get down to brass tacks?" I asked.

Georgis got up and went over to the window. Corder followed him. They whispered for a couple of minutes. They came back and took their seats.

"What do you have to swap?" Georgis asked.

"Okay, let's not nitpick. I'll give you everything I have and you do the same," I said.

"We want Greenburg's killers,"Georgis said coldly.

"I know standard procedure is for an agent to keep an hourly log during any field operation. I need to know where Kermit went and who he talked to on the day of his death," I said before they changed their minds.

"In the last couple of years, the policy is for a call-in report every two to four hours, depending on how hot the case is. Costillo has permanent hot status. It's an open investigation. Agent Greenburg was the bureau contact with our deepest cover agent within the Costillo organization. His first meeting that day was with this undercover agent. It was a scheduled meeting, the contents of which we weren't able to determine because of the shooting. Deep-cover meets are never part of standard log entries. Next he talked with a surveillance expert named Jerry Heckler. He's free-lance. The bureau has used him a couple of times on a contract basis. His last log entry said he met with a Drucilla Evers. She's a professor of economics at the University of Houston." He put his small notebook away and looked at me as if to say, your turn.

"Did he log in the reason or results of the meetings with Heckler and Evers?" I asked.

"No. He tagged the meetings CFO," he said.

The CFO tag meant for confidential files only. No standard report mode would be used. Had he lived, he would've written out the reports in question and filed them personally in a classified memory bank.

I explained the initial contact with Kermit. I covered the two murders and their connection with Costillo. I told them

153

Kermit had probably set up the meeting with me so that he could tell me something he'd learned. "Either the Costillo people were on to me in Houston and had me followed, which I doubt very much, or Kermit got hit because of someone or something he stumbled onto the day of his killing," I reasoned, as much for me as for them. "I need to know the purposes of his three meetings."

Georgis and Corder both looked a little squeamish at that request. I thought for a moment they were having second thoughts about giving me the information.

"We've . . . uh . . . we've got a little problem there," Georgis said, clearing his voice. "This morning Heckler was found dead in his workshop." He paused and sighed noticeably as he avoided looking at me. "The Evers woman was killed in a one-car accident last night. We never got a chance to talk to either of them."

This was developing into one bloody fucking case. The body count was becoming staggering. Allusoto's description of these people was right on target.

"For the record, what kind of car wreck was the Evers woman killed in?" I asked.

"She went over a bridge railing and into Buffalo Bayou. She had a nasty bump on her head and water in her lungs," he said with a touch of sarcasm in his voice.

"That leaves the informant," I said. "Want to tell me how he died last night. . . . No, let me guess. The informant is dead too. They found him shot a half-dozen times in the head with a bolt-action rifle and the local coroner called it self-inflicted."

Corder snickered under his breath.

"Our plant has a surfacing procedure. If he feels threatened or compromised, he goes into deeper cover. Any contact is totally up to him. We haven't heard a word since the shooting. Kermit was his primary contact. . . . I think he's probably fishbait." Georgis closed his notebook.

The way this was shaping up, there was a good chance that their man was now an undercover agent in the most literal sense. The only question was, did they pick up on

Kermit before or after he met with the agent? If it was before, the man was dead. If it was after, he might still be alive, but unavailable for our purposes, for who knows how long.

"There's a chance they know about you, too," he said with a hint of concern.

"One last thing," I said. "Kermit spoke to me before he died. Didn't say much, just a few fragments." I filled them in on all of the words and phrases.

The look of total surprise on their faces confirmed my suspicions that they had been given an incomplete report by HPD.

"Any idea who Gutterman is?" I asked.

They both shook their heads. They asked about the last word, and I told them I wasn't even sure of the proper spelling. We tied up a few loose ends and they told me they would run the information through the agency computer and get back to me if anything turned up. Georgis walked briskly out of the room. Corder stopped and shook my hand. "Get a big gun—a really big gun—and watch your ass. Oh yeah, one more thing, it's a good thing your friend's secretary has a great ass, 'cause she can't take a lick of shorthand."

Case walked over to the window and watched them load up and leave. He repacked his jaw and came over and sat on the edge of the table.

"It don't take no genius to figger out what's goin' on here. The Mexes are cleanin' house and gettin' rid of botherances. Problem is, you and sweetcakes here appear to me to be loose ends. Nothin' personal, honey," he said, looking at Beth. She smiled like a teacher dealing with a learning-disabled student.

He was finally forced to accept my theory about the Wilson murder. But under the circumstances, that wasn't a lot of consolation.

"What we gonna do next?" Case asked as if he didn't harbor much hope of an optimistic answer.

"The way I figure it, we're probably dead if we stop digging. Our best chance is to get hard evidence in place. Enough to force Costillo to focus his attention elsewhere. Enough to

155

make us too hot to hit. They key has to be in the name Stephen Gutterman and whatever the hell 'lemure' is."

"We best put a man with y'all all the time," he said as he mulled the situation over.

"I appreciate the thought, but I doubt it would accomplish much more than getting him killed. These guys are pro hitters. They'd take out your man without breaking stride. What would that do for me except put his family on my conscience?" I said, thinking about the possibilities. "Tell you what, though, put a man with Beth for a while. She's going to do some research for us and I think she's safer the less I'm around her."

Case didn't look entirely satisfied with my suggestions about police protection. "Besides, Allusoto gave me a gun," I said, opening my coat and exposing the pistol.

"Lord almighty, Fowler, do you remember how to use that thing?" he asked while rubbing his eyes in disbelief. "Boy, you're liable to blow your dick off as not."

"I'm not that good a shot," I replied.

"What do you make of the people Greenburg met on the day of the shooting?" Beth asked, ignoring our banter altogether. "Even though we can't question them, there must be something we can deduce from their specialties or the sequence in which he met each of them."

"That same thought has occurred to me. Why don't you head over to the college library and see if you come up with anything on Gutterman or 'lemure'? I'm going to my office and make a couple of calls and play with what we have a little," I said, getting up. Beth nodded in agreement and started to leave with me.

"I'll have Lester go with you, sweetcakes," Case said, picking up the phone. "While y'all are doin' whatever it is you do, I'll run all this shit through the East Tex Law Enforcement Computer System and see what it has to say."

We agreed to meet at Tommy's at six. I drove back to the house and picked up the school car. Beth and Lester drove my car and I took the school machine back to the security lot.

I went straight into my office, took a Coke from the fridge,

156

and put the new information on the board. I stepped back and tried to process it. I called Hob.

"Hob . . . this is Fowler. I'm okay. Yeah, it was a shitty situation. He was a good friend. No, look, I'll fill you in on all the details later. Right now I need some information about someone in your field. Do you know anything about an economics professor at the University of Houston named Drucilla Evers?" I asked.

"She's an expert on multinational corporations and that sort of thing. I've got her latest book around here somewhere if you want to read it," he offered.

"Sounds like fun reading but I'll pass on it right now," I said, thinking about what he'd told me. "By the way, the woman was killed last night in a car wreck."

There was a pause on the other end. I've always found silence on a phone to have an almost sinister quality.

"What's this all about?" he asked in a confused voice.

"I'm not sure. When I have some idea, I'll get back with you and we'll talk it over." I hung up before he could ask me anything else.

What would an expert on multinational corporations have to do with an electronics expert and a Mafia undercover agent? It was likely that Heckler had someone under surveillance, but who? What did one, or all, of these people tell Kermit to get him sufficiently alarmed to set up an urgent meeting with me? I wished to hell I understood his last words better.

Then a thought came to me. It would make sense for Esteban to put K. Brad Turrow under intense surveillance. That would explain why the hits were unsuccessful. The odds against thwarting two pro hits in a row, without prior information, are real small. But why kill Heckler if he was providing the surveillance? For that matter, why Kermit? What had Heckler found out that mandated his execution?

The phone rang. It was an excited Beth. "Fowler, stay right where you are. I'll be there in a minute," she said, bursting at the seams. "I know what Greenburg was trying to tell you." With that she hung up.

I sat back and tried to figure out what she might've found in the library that would break this case. When she came into the office, she had the look of a woman who had recently been Fowlerized. Well, at least she looked happy.

"We should be getting a long distance call in just a minute," she said with a smile. "I left your extension with Anson's office."

"You left my extension with your husband's office. Why does that bother me?" I asked.

"Probably because you've a prehistoric conception of marital fidelity combined with a typical male notion of the wronged husband reaction," she explained.

"Oh, I see. No one's ever explained it to me before," I replied rather weakly. I knew there was an insult in there somewhere.

"Fowler, not only will I get a thesis out of this, but you'll get a Pulitzer, too," she said, opening her briefcase and dumping its contents on my desk. "This is even bigger than we thought." She placed a copy of a *Houston Chronicle* article in front of me. It was three years old. "Read the underlined paragraphs," she suggested.

It was an article depicting the ongoing plight of the Texas Department of Corrections. A federal district judge had ruled that the state's penal system was overcrowded to the point where the civil rights of the inmates were being violated. The federal judge, whose name was William Justice of all things, ordered the system to refuse additional inmates until the facilities were expanded. I remembered the story. It had even been the source of some conversation at a couple of the poker games. I didn't see the connection to the case. I was about to say as much when another article found its way on the top of the last. It was the same year as the first one, but was from the *Austin American*. It seems that Governor Clements had decided to violate yet another campaign promise and build several new prisons to relieve the overcrowding and restore order to the penal system. If there's anything worse than a lame-duck governor, it has to be a ruptured-duck governor. Anyway, among the facilities to be constructed was one which would be the most advanced maximum-security prison in the nation. It would house up to six thousand inmates, only the most violent offenders. I remembered something of this prison. The damn thing was built near Morrisville.

"Will there be a vocabulary test that ties into this reading?" I said.

She smiled. "Are you losing interest here? Consider these articles foreplay," she suggested.

On top of the second article fell a third. This one was uptown all the way. It was a copy of a *U.S. News & World Report*. It tied the whole thing together. The story followed the Texas Department of Corrections' search for a company to build their high-tech prison of the future. The state had finally selected a Swedish firm called Worldco. The multinational construction company had significantly underbid the competitors, according to a high-ranking state official. In addition to their low bid, the company had hired renowned prison architect Stephen Gutterman. It was like a light went on in my head. Things were falling into place.

"There's more on the last page," she said, turning the page and watching my reaction.

It seems our Mr. Gutterman had originally gained fame for his construction of a high-tech maximum-security facility outside the French city of Lemur.

The phone rang. It was someone in Anson's office calling for Beth. She listened for a couple of minutes, then hung up with the look of someone who had just swallowed a canary.

"Let me guess," I said, putting up my hand to stop her from finishing her explanation of the call. "You've just discovered that Worldco is owned by K. Brad Turrow."

"Oh . . . that's very good. That's better than very good. Very few men of your age would've figured that out," she chided with a mischievous smile.

"It explains both Kermit's death and Heckler's death." I walked over and put the information on the board with the other data. I stood back from the board and looked thoughtfully at the data.

"Why don't you explain it to me as you see it," I suggested.

"All right, we've got one pissed-off billionaire when Paco gets life. He tries to have him killed and is unsuccessful more than once. Esteban convinces K. Brad to find another hobby. K. Brad wises up and tries an end run. He gets control of the very prison where Paco will be housed. My guess is that he has somehow designed the prison with a way to get at Paco." She finished her description and searched for some sign of approval.

"How does our theory explain the killings of Kermit, Heckler, and the Evers woman?"

She got up and walked around the room a couple of times. If she had been sitting across from me at a poker game, I'd have said she was about to play a marginal hand.

"Let's say that the informant, in the Costillo organization tells Kermit that the family has Turrow under surveillance. The informant tells Kermit Heckler is doing it for them. Depending on how long Turrow had been under surveillance, they would know about us." She paused and thought for a moment. "Greenburg goes to Heckler and confronts him with what he's just discovered. It turns out that Heckler has been holding out on Costillo. Maybe he plans to sell his information to the highest bidder. I don't know. Anyway, Kermit is able to get the information from Heckler. He goes to the Evers woman to confirm the connection between Worldco and K. Brad Turrow. It's a honeymoon fit if I ever saw one," she said with total confidence.

While listening to Beth, I had come to a realization that bothered me greatly. Was Kermit dead because I'd mentioned our association to Turrow at the meeting? Was that the point at which the Costillo people first became aware of this involvement? I was sickened by the prospect, but this wasn't the time for guilt. I'd deal with it later.

"That's not bad, lady," I said as positively as I could. "If Heckler was tapped into the Turrow organization, he must have made me not later than the meeting with K. Brad. They made Kermit either from something I said to Turrow or from some of his digging. They assumed he was trying to foul up their plan to release Paco. They followed Kermit to the informant, then to Evers. When they saw him meeting with Heckler they must have figured Heckler was planning some sort of double cross. They probably weren't sure how all these people fit into our scheme, so they just erased the lot. You know . . . it's just possible that Heckler didn't tell them about K. Brad's plan. They may have killed him before he had a chance to bargain with the information. From what the agents told us, it sounds like Heckler had been around. If so, he would've known that telling them what he knew wouldn't save his life. They'd be even more pissed that he had held out and endangered Paco. There's a real chance that he bought the farm with a smile on his face, knowing that Paco was doomed. If that's the case, then the plan is still a go."

"If they were on to you from the Turrow meeting on, how is it that they missed you at the bar?" she asked.

"I don't know," I answered. "Maybe the hitters weren't the surveillance people. Maybe, from where the shooters were located, the guy at the bar resembled me. I doubt we'll ever know for sure."

"There are some gray areas, but all in all, it's a good fit," she said, thinking it over as she looked at the board.

"With every dawning there follows a darkening," I said. "What do we do now? Can we allow K. Brad Turrow to go through with his plan?" I asked.

"There is that," Beth replied. "You realize of course that once again we've got story material, but probably not court-quality evidence here. Which means that we might be able to stop the release, but we've no guarantee that anyone's going to pay the freight for the carnage," she said with some bitterness in her tone.

"Are you suggesting," I countered, "that we allow Paco Costillo to be executed by Turrow's people?"

"I'm not suggesting anything. I'm just stating facts," she replied.

The temptation was great to let Turrow exact his measure of justice. It was time to leave for dinner with Case. We three would have to discuss these things more thoroughly later.

20

Trouble in Mayberry

I FELT SILLY AS hell carrying a gun. I had it pushed as far to the back of my pants as possible.

"You know something?" she asked without expectation of reply. "I'm hungry enough to eat almost anything. I plan on being an expensive date this evening."

"Is that a fact?" I said. "You should know that in east Texas, when a man spends more than two dollars on a wench, it's customary for her to show her appreciation by doing some little something in violation of the state's sodomy laws."

"Hold that thought," she teased.

Case wasn't there yet. We ordered something to drink and settled down for a few minutes of relaxation. Beth ordered some German beer in honor of Mr. Gutterman. I ordered a Diet Coke in honor of my thirst.

Our conversation was interrupted by the loud, obnoxious bellowing of our mayor, Ed Andy. Unfortunately for everyone in earshot, the semimonthly meeting of the local chamber of commerce was a few minutes from starting. They used the banquet room of Tommy's for their meetings. Ed Andy and several of the local political players were camped at the bar and putting on a show. Ed Andy was already shit-faced. When he got that way, he became belligerent. This night he was recalling the past glories of the Fightin' Nighthawks. Specifically, the 1967 edition of the Nacogdoches High School football team. It was a team on which he had starred. It was also the only local team ever to make it to the championship game of the state tournament.

"We woulda won that damn championship if they hadn't

killed our nigger," he proclaimed loudly. He was referring to the fact that the 1967 team had the first-ever black player. Before that, the town had one white school and one black school. We used to call it separate but unequal. The black kid's name was Odibee Edmonds. He was the fastest kid in the county. Some said he got that way by stealing hubcaps and running away on foot. The year before, he had placed second in the state in the hundred yard dash. I still think he would've won the race if they'd allowed him to carry a wire wheel. Anyway, he broke his arm in the first quarter of the tournament game. Without Odibee, the Nacogdoches offense fizzled.

"We killed their nigger, too," Ed Andy said proudly amidst a chorus of belches from the listeners. He shook his head sadly. "Them sneaky sons of bitches had themselves another nigger. By the time we killed him, they'd scored too many points."

The drunken display of racism was embarrassing standing by itself. The fact that one of our black professors and his wife were seated not two booths from the bar magnified Ed Andy's lunacy. The elderly and distinguished philosophy professor slowly escorted his wife from the place. They passed with quiet elegance before the offending horde, or herd, as the case may be. Directly in front of Ed Andy, they stopped, and the professor took off his glasses and put them away. He looked at Ed Andy with sadness in his eyes.

"Fuck you and the horse you rode in on, buttwipe," he said with impeccable diction and left. I've always thought that the essence of communication is proper encoding.

Ed was so stunned that he couldn't even muster up any gas. He'd just been destroyed by Uncle Ben.

"Gee, Fowler, I don't understand why you and the mayor don't get along better. Philosophically speaking, you're two peas in a pod," Beth said, chuckling under her breath.

"What a quaint, folksy metaphor . . . especially for a city girl," I responded with due sarcasm.

"Tell me something. How does he get elected, given the number of black people in this town?"

163

"There are plenty of blacks all right, but they aren't politically active. They're throwbacks to the fifties. I keep hoping that one day soon they'll figure out this voting business and send that bloated, bilious bastard back to selling pickups." We toasted the thought.

In the middle of the toast, Case slid into the booth beside Beth. "How long has Ed Andy been holdin' court?" he asked.

"Long enough to explain for the hundredth time his views on why we lost the state championship," I replied.

Case offered no comment. He pulled the plug from his pocket and, at the same time, motioned to the waitress, who promptly delivered a setter to the table. He was in mid-bite when he caught sight of Beth's horrified expression. He unhappily put the plug away intact but vented his anxiety by killing the setter with one mighty drink. He told the waitress to keep him supplied.

"I busted my ass on the computer and came up as dry as a prairie-dog fart. I didn't find doodly-squat," he growled.

We spent the next hour and a half discussing what Beth had uncovered. Case wasn't convinced that Turrow was planning to get at Paco through the prison. It was too farfetched. He'd seen the prison. It was impressive. The personnel were state people now. He argued that Turrow's people had no access. I told him that we were going to see Turrow and confront him with what we had. If nothing else, it would keep us moving and harder for the Costillo people to find.

It was twilight when we all left. Case was parked a couple of spaces in front of us. We were almost to my car when a couple of figures moved from the shadows to our left. Even half drunk, Case was cat-quick. I don't know if he saw their guns or just sensed their intentions. Whichever, he pushed Beth and me down beside a car. He dove forward, pulling his gun as he fell. At the same time all this was happening, the two men opened fire at us. It was eerie. Their weapons made no loud sounds. There were simply bright flashes coming from the barrels. They hadn't gotten as close to us as they had wanted. It's hard to say how many shots they fired before Case was in position to return fire. I heard the window shatter above my head. I saw a couple of slugs tear into the fender of my car. I pushed Beth toward the rear of the car we were lying next to and told her to crawl off in the other direction and hide. I reached for the gun in my belt. By this time Case was on one knee returning fire. He missed. I saw him get hit high in the shoulder and spin onto the hood of a Firebird. I heard him groan as another bullet hit him in the thigh. He fell to the ground as the two killers walked toward us. I could see their feet from under the car. I prepared myself for the confrontation, took a deep breath, and stood up with the gun poised for action. To my dismay, they weren't there anymore. Well, that's not entirely true. They were there. They were, however, lying motionless on the ground. I instinctively crouched down and surveyed the area. There was no one around. This didn't make any sense. I hadn't fired at all and Case's efforts had missed. I hadn't heard any other gunfire either. I slowly walked toward the first of the prone men. I kept my gun on him all the time. Beth came back, picked up Case's revolver, and followed me.

The first man was lying facedown on the pavement. I kicked the automatic away from the outstretched hand. I put my gun to his head and slowly rolled him over. Beth kept her gun aimed at the other one while I was doing this. He had a hole the size of a dime in the middle of his forehead. It was amazingly neat, with very little blood.

The other one was lying on his back. His face was expressionless. He might've been lying there looking at the heavens had it not been for the hole almost perfectly between the eyes.

We moved immediately to Case. By this time, he was trying to pull himself up onto the fender of the Firebird. He was bleeding like a stuck pig. Beth and I helped him onto the hood. She made a tourniquet from my belt and slowed the blood flow from the more serious of the two wounds. Once the belt was firmly around his leg, she tore off part of her shirt and began to work on his shoulder. It was then we heard the sirens.

"Fowler," he said as he sat up on the hood and surveyed

the area, "goddamn, you did good." He was in considerable pain and had already lost a good deal of blood. I decided not to go into any details right then.

As the paramedics were treating him, he was giving out instructions right and left. He refused sedation until he had control of the scene.

"I told my people to get you two home right away. You need to get on out of here before the state and county boys get here and tie you up all night." He grimaced with pain. "I figure y'all will be all right the rest of tonight. They don't usually send no second team. I'll have a man stay the night in your driveway. It can't hurt nothin'." The attendant motioned for us to get out of there so they could get Case to the hospital. They finally started to the ambulance.

"One more thing . . . don't be followin' me to the hospital. My happy ass will be chasin' Dolly Parton in ten minutes. If I did wake up, I sure as hell wouldn't want to see your ugly goddamn puss. . . . Sweetcakes . . . you did real fine tonight." Either he passed out or they had managed to sedate him without his knowing it.

I had my arm around Beth. We stood there and watched the ambulance drive away. Dewey Torence, Case's second-in-command, came over to us. Beth still had Case's gun in her hand. She had forgotten all about it. Dewey took it from her gently.

"Fowler, that's the best fuckin' shootin' I've ever seen," he said, looking at the two corpses. "'Scuse my language, ma'am."

"Don't look at me, Dewey," I said, acting surprised. "It was Case who shot them. He fired off two rounds as he was falling. It was amazing. He dropped them like ducks," I said. He looked at Beth and she nodded in agreement.

"But the chief said . . ." He was starting to protest when I handed him my gun. He stopped talking and took the weapon.

"See for yourself, it hasn't been fired," I argued.

He smelled the muzzle and checked the clip. He then looked at Case's gun.

166

"I'll be a son of a bitch if there ain't but two slugs missin'. Two shots . . . two head hits . . . that's somethin'. . . . But why did he say. . . ?" he started to ask.

"I don't believe he knows he did it. He was wounded so badly that he just reacted instinctively," I explained.

As we drove away I looked around the area. I knew someone was out there watching us.

"Still trying to work off those ducks?" she asked.

I knew when the news hit the street about a real shoot-out right here in Nacogdoches with a couple of real bad boys, it'd capture the people's imagination for weeks. Around here the best possible reelection scenario is a shoot-out where the bad guys buy the farm and the good guy does some hospital time. It kept John Wayne in Mexican women and beans for fifty years and it might get Case reelected another term or two.

"Won't the ballistic reports prove that it wasn't Case's gun that killed them?" she asked.

"They might, then again they might not. Most of the time when a slug enters the head, it gets flattened and smashed. Usually it's almost impossible to get a match. Hell, anyway, by the time all this is cleared up, Case will be in office and his legend intact."

"Who shot them?" she asked as she looked behind us.

"Lady, I wish I knew. It's not the bureau's style. But, the murder of an agent, especially one as popular as Kermit, might generate some maverick behavior," I said as I turned off Main Street. Beth sat quietly. "On the other hand, it could be Turrow's people or even some players we don't know about. . . . Whoever they were, we owe them one," I offered.

I could feel her looking at me. I turned and looked at her. She was smiling.

"Care to explain that particular smile?" I asked.

"No," she replied. "However, something was said earlier this evening about east Texas traditions."

I speeded up.

21

The Angels of Justice

AT 8:00 A.M. SHARP I dialed the private number Turrow had given us at our last meeting. An assistant answered the phone, but yielded it quickly to K. Brad. He was as cordial as ever. I told him that we needed to meet again. He asked no questions and suggested that the meeting take place in his offices in Dallas around two o'clock. He offered to have us flown to Dallas. I told him we'd drive.

I sat there with my hand on the receiver for a few seconds.

"What's wrong?" Beth asked from her perch on the bed. She was wearing only a smile, sitting Indian style.

"In his shoes, I'd have had a few questions . . . unless of course, I already had the answers or the questions didn't matter." I never finished the train of thought. The ringing phone shifted my mind's eye.

It was Dewey calling to tell me that Case was all right. He'd be in the hospital a spell, but was on the mend. He also had a preliminary report on one of the hitmen. He had been a member of the Costillo organization and had a long and violent history.

"Have you been interviewed about the shooting?" I asked.

"You bet your sweet ass I have," he replied cheerfully. "By this time tomorrow Case Bayhill will be as famous as Bufford Pussy," he predicted with confidence.

"That's Pusser, not pussy," I informed him.

"Whatever. The election oughta be a lock," he boldly proclaimed.

"I hope you're right," I said with more reserve. "By the way, you can take your man off us this morning. We're leaving for Dallas in a few minutes. Maybe we can get out of here before the local reporters swarm the place looking for information about last night."

"Y'all be careful, ya hear?" he said, hanging up.

"Fowler, what are we going to do if K. Brad denies the whole thing?" she asked.

"I don't know. Any suggestions?" I asked.

"Not really. I've done some thinking about his situation. I have a sense of his loss. I wouldn't want to ruin his reputation, or worse, over the likes of Paco Costillo." She sounded as if she was thinking out loud.

It was a question I had asked myself a couple of times in the last several hours.

"If we're forced to go public and K. Brad is hurt by the effort, keep a couple of things clear in your mind. First, it'll be his choice. We're going to give him an opportunity to walk away from this intact. Secondly, if we go public, it won't be for Paco Costillo, it'll be for the system. I can't see anything but chaos coming from a situation where anybody with power can define and orchestrate their own version of justice."

"I guess," she said, getting up and moving around for the first time that morning. It would be fair to say that Beth hadn't exactly embraced my explanation with her full and enthusiastic support. I didn't blame her. The words were true, the concept valid, but the consequences nauseating. A no-win situation at best.

"How would you like to make a slight detour through Morrisville on our way to Dallas?" I asked.

"That might prove to be interesting," she replied. "How far out of our way is the prison?"

"About an hour, but I'm interested in seeing the damn thing," I explained. "It represents the most expensive hit in history."

"I'm a little curious too about a two-hundred-million-dollar, escape-proof prison that will house six thousand killers," she said, heading for the kitchen.

"There's one other thing," I said. "Somewhere this side of Dallas, I want to rent a car so that when I meet with K. Brad you can be tucked away somewhere else. Before you have a shit hemorrhage, this doesn't have anything to do with protecting you as a woman. It protects us both. As a matter of fact, I wouldn't meet with K. Brad if I didn't have a trump card in reserve. Look, we both like the man, but it's impossible to know what the pressures of all this have done to his mind. If we're right, he's spent millions of dollars to build a prison just to kill one man. As good a man as he's been up till now, we can't be sure that this obsession for revenge hasn't warped him completely. He could be as dangerous to us with respect to his plan as Esteban Costillo is with his."

"That makes sense," she acknowledged.

"I thought we'd rent a car and have you stay at a motel somewhere out of reach. We'll have a time frame set up whereby you'll automatically contact the authorities if I don't contact you," I said, formulating the plan as I talked.

"Do you really think we have something to fear from Turrow?" she asked, hoping I'd say no.

"Who knows? But the stakes have gotten too high to play fast and loose," I told her.

In the morning light, I developed a whole new perspective on the events of the previous night. My car looked like it had been in a war zone. There were two bullet holes in the left-front fender. The driver's side window was shattered. I made sure I had the gun.

We cruised through a local fast-food establishment and suffered through a generic breakfast. While there, I called the hospital and checked on Case. The nurse told me he was out of danger and resting well. She said he was sleeping with a smile on his face. He must have caught up with Dolly a couple of times.

It's about two and a half hours to Morrisville. The drive from Nacogdoches is all two-lane, mostly farm-to-market roads. The pace was leisurely as we passed through a dozen or so small east-Texas towns, all with populations of less than a thousand. About an hour out, we stopped at a combination convenience store and gas station. Every one of these little towns has one of these establishments just off

170

the main highway. This one had gas, groceries, Canton melons, fast food, and live minnows. If they added a bar and a whorehouse, a man wouldn't ever have to leave.

We had just crested a hill when we spotted him. A lone man was walking slowly along the roadside dragging a cross. Actually, as we got closer, we discovered that he was half pulling and half dragging the cross. On the burying end there was a wheel.

"As a good Catholic girl, do you remember whether or not the original cross had a wheel on the end?" I asked.

She assured me that such had not been the case. But she did hedge her bet a little by pointing out that she had no information about the Protestant version of the events.

"Why do you suppose he's rolling the cross along the roadside as opposed to carrying it, as was the original method of transport as I recall?" she asked with a smile not indicative of heavenly thoughts.

I explained to her that Texans would do anything in the name of the church, except live according to the commandments. We concluded this probably wasn't the method used by Jesus. It must represent a figurative gesture of faith.

"Do you think he'll get where he's going?" she asked, trying to see the reaction of the occupants of another car going in the other direction.

"It's six to five that he gets pelted with beer cans by at least two carloads of drunken college students, the wheel is stolen at gunpoint as he nears a town of any size, and if he makes it to Dibol, they'll ticket him for speeding," I said with the conviction of a cynic.

The sign said MORRISVILLE CORRECTIONAL FACILITY NEXT RIGHT. Texas has always maintained one of the largest prison populations in the nation. There are a number of reasons for this, not the least of which is the Baptist lobby, which has succeeded in making illegal almost everything enjoyable. Texas likes to locate its penal facilities as far from the madding crowd as possible. Years ago, a decision was reached that the prisons ought to be self-supporting. Thus a major rehabilitative innovation was introduced called the pea patch. For years the prisons were referred to as the pea farm. I had seen many of these facilities through the years. But I'd never seen anything quite like Morrisville.

The facility was enormous. It stood out from the rural surroundings like a Steven Spielberg production. It was acres of steel, stone, brick, and glass. It was new and it was gleaming. If I hadn't known it was a prison, I might have mistaken it for a science complex of some sort. There was not a barred window to be seen from the outside. None of the customary razor wire atop the walls. The entire complex was surrounded by an ornate stone and ornamental iron fence. The parking lot was paved, lighted, and landscaped. As a final touch to the facility, it had a tourist station, a small building outside the fence that accessed the parking lot. I couldn't believe it, so I went in. Inside were all the specifications of the prison. There was a listing and explanation of all of its high-tech characteristics. There was a scaled-down mock-up on a table in the middle of the room. The usual plaques decorated the walls. There were Morrisville T-shirts and glasses. I thought about suggesting a T-shirt slogan for them: We who are about to die are seriously pissed.

I wondered what sort of family would visit an area just to see a prison. Then it came to me—out-of-state Baptists, of course. Bill Clement's name was stamped on everything but the toilet paper in the men's room. There must be irony somewhere in that. Beth and I invested fifteen minutes in a short film chronicling the construction of the facility. We got our first look at the once-mysterious Stephen Gutterman, complete with hard hat. All in all, it was an interesting experience.

We drove around the facility as much as the access roads would allow. In the rear of the complex was a road to a gate that was used for inmate transfer. It was lined on both sides by oak trees. I thought it strange that all of the trees were either dead or dying. In Texas, oaks grow like grass. Even stranger was the gate at the end of the road. There was a large stone arch under which inmates had to pass. On either side of the arch were large stone angels. These weren't your standard angels. They were in gowns and had wings, but they also had horrific expressions on their faces. They had almost a gargoyle effect. The entire facility left me feeling cold. Beth saw me studying the angels.

"They're the angels of justice . . . as opposed to angels of mercy," she said.

"What was that?" I asked, not having been paying full attention.

"According to the brochure, they're the angels of justice," she reiterated. "They're patterned after the angels of an old legend. Supposedly they served as guards at the gate separating heaven and hell."

I thought it odd that an ultra-modern facility like this would have an almost Gothic nook tucked away from easy view.

We drove on to the Dallas airport and rented Beth a car. We went over our schedule and the logistics of meeting later that evening. She was to get a room at the Airport Ramada Inn and await my call by six o'clock. If I didn't call, she was to contact the police and tell them where I was. I left her the gun and told her to drive for a while and try to lose any possible tail.

22

Impact Defined

W HEN THE PRICE OF West Texas crude started to drop in the early eighties, so, it seemed, did the IQs of the legions of Texas millionaires, who only a few months before had all appeared to be Rhodes scholars. The vast majority of the fortunes in this state were based on a simple truth: There will always be a demand for oil. In addition to that indisputable, almost ordained truth, the logistics of the oil business appealed to the average Texan immensely. Just poke a hole in the ground and let nature's bounty escape. Since most Texans will poke anything, the industry was a natural. Unfortunately, this, like most simple truths, was too simple to be really true. It turned out that demand, in the absence of price stability, was a weak foundation for a state's economy. We'd allowed the local oil industry to inflate to the point where a twenty-dollar-plus barrel price was necessary to do business profitably. The shit hit the fan when those historically ignorant and always godless Arabs figured all this out. These "sand niggers," as they were commonly called during the arrogance of the boom, started to invest their untold billions into hundreds of non-oil-related industries. They then glutted the market with cheap oil. It ruined the intellectuals in our area, but the ignorant heathens prospered because of their diversification. Your basic Texas millionaire reacted to falling oil prices by investing in real estate, oil-field equipment, and larger, more extravagant houses. The result was a state in economic chaos.

Rising above all this fiscal and intellectual mediocrity was K. Brad Turrow. He'd seen it all coming. The real players always do. Before the worst happened, he expanded his busi-

174

ness interests into high-potential, non-oil-related ventures. He had a Midas touch. He'd actually gotten richer during the hard times. He lived and officed in Turrow Towers. These twin fifty-six-story buildings were the focal points of the storied Dallas skyline. Their blue-green marble-and-glass exteriors were the most aesthetically pleasing edifices in the area.

K. Brad occupied the top floor of the Romulus Tower. I thought that odd, given the legend, but what was normal anymore? I figured the Garden of Eden had to be something like this. The lobby was eight or ten stories tall. There were trees, fountains, large boulders, and waterfalls in the middle. All the offices on the first eight floors or so looked out on it.

As per my instructions, I went to the information desk on level one of the lobby. I gave my name to the young lady in charge and was told someone would be with me in a minute. In about that amount of time I was confronted by a man in his forties who looked and smelled like an executive for a large company. He introduced himself as Andrew Capers, assistant to K. Brad Turrow. The handshake was perfunctory, the smile was surgically formed, and the name definitely wasn't Andy. He had a clammy quality to him. I sensed that he was probably coldly efficient and Eastern educated. I wondered if Harvard offered a combination business and mortuary degree. He directed me to a private elevator that required a key. The inside of the elevator was posh, with leather seating.

The doors opened directly into a huge room. The far walls were glass, with a balcony on the other side. North Dallas was at our feet. The seating area was sunken four steps. It was furnished with exotic fabrics and ass-deep carpet. I wanted to dislike the room, but I couldn't. It had a clean elegance that dulled the offensiveness of its opulence. Sitting behind a desk off in a corner was K. Brad Turrow. He was reading something with his full attention. He looked up and Andrew nodded and left. K. Brad got up and moved over to one of the large sofas.

"Have a seat, Fowler. I'm glad you could come." He sounded sincere. "Can I get you something to drink?"

175

"Something soft with a lot of ice," I replied as I took a seat. I was feeling a rush of the type you might get playing poker for stakes you couldn't afford.

He handed me the drink and sat down across from me on another sofa. He was wearing half-glasses and a couple of thousand dollars' worth of casual clothes.

"So, Fowler . . . to what do I owe this visit?" he asked with the air of a man meeting a good friend for the first time in a while.

"Well, hell, K. Brad, I think you're planning to kill Paco Costillo. I think your plan has to do with the Morrisville prison facility, which was constructed by a company you own." I sipped hard on the Coke and watched his face. "I suspect that it's a plan that has been in the works for some time. That would explain your seeming timidity upon hearing of Esteban's plan to free the boy back in Nacogdoches."

"That's an interesting story. It would make for a fascinating novel, I suspect," he said without concern.

"Okay, we'll play out the hand," I said, never taking my eyes from him. "But, understand something. I'm not going to let it happen, if I can help it. I don't have certifiable court-room-quality evidence. What I do have is a hell of a lot of the circumstantial stuff that reporters crave. I'm pretty sure I can get someone to print what I've got."

"Frankly, assuming you really believe all this, I'm puzzled as to why you're not out there heralding your message right now," he said calmly.

"Maybe I have a sense of your grief . . . maybe I just plain like you . . . bottom line is I want you to call a halt to this lunacy before I'm forced to cause you harm," I answered.

He took off his glasses and laid them on the table at his side. He walked over to the windows that overlooked Dallas. Without turning around, he started to talk. "It's amazing how easy it is to get rich, to accumulate things. There was a time, not too long ago, when that was important to me. Then one day it came to me that the only really important elements of my life were a few people who meant everything to me. My wife, my son, and his family became the nucleus of my existence. Then Paco Costillo murdered the largest part of me. I didn't know how to deal with it at first. I sought justice through the court system. Early on, it was made clear to me that people like Paco are seldom held accountable for their butchery. The legal system isn't capable of dealing with the Pacos of the world. My wife, in a fit of desperation, had a stroke. It left her paralyzed and comatose. Paco was killing the rest of me while in prison. I found an irony in that death. It affords one a curious amount of freedom," he said, continuing to survey the Dallas skyline.

The rush was gone. Reality had taken its place. There was too much pain in the man to allow any more cat-and-mouse games.

"For a man of your position to lower himself to the level of a Costillo *is* lunacy. You've built an empire within the context of the system. Until you were personally burned, the system seemed good enough to you. All right, it doesn't always work as fairly and efficiently as we'd like. Imperfect as it is, it's still necessary for the provision of something approaching order. Without it we are less. The laws are the glue. . . . As much as I admire you, I can't lower myself with you." I was still hopeful of a crack in his armor.

He turned slowly from his window refuge and looked into my eyes. "What was it you said back in Nacogdoches? 'I'm not sure the legal system offers any real hope of seeing justice fulfilled here'—or something to that effect. Now you tell me that the system doesn't always work as fairly and efficiently as we'd like. You do turn a nice, neat phrase, Fowler. . . . But let's cut through the bullshit, shall we? Let's see now . . . Paco Costillo kills a prostitute, my son, my daughter-in-law, and my granddaughter. He's found guilty beyond a reasonable doubt. I guess his still being alive falls under the category of a little inefficiency. But let's go on. His father has a woman killed in your town. A young woman is murdered by them in Houston. Not satisfied, the Costillo people kill an FBI agent, an off-duty policeman, and an innocent bystander unlucky enough to be at the wrong place at the wrong time. The legal system that serves as the glue will never bring the old man to justice. The magnitude of the atrocity will be increased by the fact that the murders of these people will serve as part of a plan to gain the release of Paco." He paused as he neared the sofa where I was sitting. He placed the palms of his hands together with the fingers extended. He rested his chin on the apex for a second. "A little less fair and efficient just doesn't say it for me."

There was enough truth in his words to make what I had thought to be an untenable position seem almost reasonable.

"How could we survive if every person who felt wronged took the law into his own hands?" I asked.

"We're not talking about every person. We're talking about me in this one situation. To attack my proposition by generalizing beyond its parameters is fallacy. Judge the act on its merits alone. . . . But hypothetically let's look at your question for a minute. History is full of examples where the legal system of the time failed to operate efficiently and people were forced to take measures on their own. In every case two things happened. First, the cancer was exorcised from the system. Second, the system was forced to evolve to meet future needs of this type. Hell, San Francisco would never have evolved to its present cultural status if the early vigilantes had not taken matters into their own hands and rid the area of corrupt politicians and the Barbary criminal element. It's eminently arguable that actions such as the one you reject are necessary for change." His voice was cold and his logic colder. "Let me ask you a question. How long can our society survive in any recognizable fashion, if people like the Costillo family are allowed to subvert the system at will?"

"Isn't that what you're trying to do, subvert the system to suit your purposes?" I fired back. I set my empty glass on the table. "From a systemic point of view, any subversion, whether by you or Costillo, is damaging to the system."

"Fowler, there is more value in right and wrong than there is to any system. Most systems react to the ebb and flow of those who control and worship them. There is no intrinsic value to any system beyond its ability to serve its worshipers. Even today the United Nations and the weight of two hundred years of international law can't deal with criminal nations. In this country, our legal system can't deal effectively with criminals who have enough money and power to seduce its officials on all levels. Criminality is dynamic, the legal system only grows incrementally. The system can't work," he said as he lowered his head and wiped his brow with his hand. "If I were to select any hundred people on the street below and ask them if they felt Paco Costillo ought to be executed, we both know they would overwhelmingly support his death. Why is he still alive then? It's because the system only works for people like him. . . . But then we already knew that, didn't we? Isn't that a large part of why you left the real world for the classroom? Tell me you saw the system work when you were out on the street. Isn't that what Nacogdoches is all about? The system failed to work there once, didn't it? Maureen Wilson is dead. Your best friend is in the hospital. By all rights you and your young lady friend ought to be dead. And you know, Fowler, the system couldn't stop it from happening, and it's not capable of punishing those responsible." His businesslike, calm demeanor was changing. He was getting more and more intense.

"It's a little early in the game to say for sure that the Costillo people won't be forced to pay for their crimes," I said. "With my information and your power, we might be able to jump-start the whole system. I think we're better off altering the system through process than through revenge." He was looking at a picture on the table. It was a picture of his family. "Even if everything you've said were true, how much of a difference will killing Paco Costillo make? In the larger sense, what would be the impact?"

He picked up the picture from the table and closed his eyes. He took a deep breath, placed the picture back in its place, and set his jaw.

"Did you know that my granddaughter Casey was only five years old when she was killed?" he asked with a little quiver in his voice. I didn't answer him. "The autopsy said that she died from suffocation." The pain in his eyes was overpowering. It was clear to me that anyone carrying that much pain was dangerous. "You see, they . . . ah . . . they didn't shoot her as they did her parents. They tied her up and buried her alive . . . underneath her parents' dead bodies. The coroner told me that it may have taken a half an hour for her to die in the darkness of her grave."

He sighed deeply and seemed to be trying to gather himself. "I guess impact is relative. In the eyes of the beholder," he said.

His eyes told me that pretenses was no longer important to him. He didn't admit his intention, it was simply understood between us.

"What about the rehab program? Was all that a part of the sham . . . just for camouflage to enhance your chances of getting at Paco?"

"It was an effort to deal with the realities from every possible perspective. I'm not an impulsive, vengeful megalomaniac shooting from the hip. I've tried every viable avenue to get justice. On another level, it afforded me access to the penal system and created a useful persona."

He got up and asked me to follow him. He led me to a large room off the main room. It was full of computer equipment.

"How much do you know about the Morrisville facility?" he asked as he hit a switch and a large color monitor lit up, revealing a blueprint that I recognized from the tourist room.

"Not a great deal," I said as I looked around the room. It was reminiscent of those high-tech control rooms that were integral elements of sixties spy movies. "I have seen the place once and read a little about it."

He flashed me a knowing smile and walked over to the illuminated screen. "The facility is the most technologically advanced penal institution in the world. Its surveillance capabilities are state of the art. There are virtually no blind spots in the prison. A damaging riot is impossible. At no time are more than six inmates allowed in a single confined space. At the first sign of trouble, either prisonwide or in a specific confined space, two situation stabilizing procedures are automatically activated by computer. First, all confined

180

spaces are electronically partitioned, thereby containing the prison population in small, manageable groups. Second, a newly developed sedative gas called Dythol forty-four is circulated through the unstable area or areas. It takes effect in five seconds. The situation is completely stabilized in a matter of seconds without a single guard being placed at risk. The accounting procedures, nutritional management, educational rehabilitation—all the prison functions are computerized to the point where nine people can run the entire facility at full capacity. That's six thousand inmates." He was spitting out this information at a rapid pace. It was obviously a subject he had spent some time on.

"Of course, escape is almost impossible," he continued. "My people tell me that the odds of a person beating this system and escaping are one in one hundred and fifteen thousand. There are backup electrical systems and twenty-four-hour monitoring on the entire system from a facility outside the walls. Just in case the impossible happens and there is a riot, a full company of Texas Rangers is permanently stationed in the area, outside the actual complex." He pointed to a building on the screen. "The Lemur facility has had no escapes and no population control problems in the eleven years of its operation." It was clear that the man was rightfully proud of the prison.

"It is a remarkable facility," I said honestly.

He moved from the diagram of the prison to the computer banks. He looked at them for a second, then sat on the edge of one of the terminal tables and put his glasses on.

"In these data banks are the entire case histories of all 5,216 convicted capital offenders in the state of Texas. Paco is a member of this select club. As of this morning, 5,102 of these men are presently housed in the Morrisville facility." He punched a button on the terminal nearest to him and information began to spew forth.

"Let's calculate the total impact upon society of these some five thousand men," he said, looking over the data. "Between them, these men are responsible for a minimum of 16,002 murders, 2,771 rapes, 31,256 robberies, and

11,245 assaults. We only traced these crimes. Statistics show that only two in a thousand of these men will be executed. One of two things will happen to the ones not executed. Either they will serve their remaining years in prison at a cost to the taxpayer of twelve thousand dollars per year—by the way, the average age of these people is twenty-two—or they will be released in some manner. In that instance, eighty-three percent of them will recidivate." He stopped reading from the sheet and looked at me as if he were about to overtrump my king.

Somewhere in the reading of all that data, it had hit me like a Tyson hook. It was unbelievable—almost totally beyond comprehension. K. Brad wasn't going to kill just Paco Costillo. He was planning to kill every man in the Morrisville facility, all 5,102 of them. In one mad stroke he was going to eliminate every capital offender in the state of Texas. The gas distribution system, the overwhelming expense of the project—it all came together. This wasn't just about Paco. I've played a lot of poker hands and run a few bluffs in my day, but I've never had more difficulty maintaining a poker face. It had been risky for me to approach the man with a threat to expose an attempt to kill Paco Costillo, but it would be absolute insanity for me to let him know my suspicions about this.

"So you see, Fowler, a tremendous amount of time and effort went into planning the Morrisville facility. The state of Texas will benefit greatly from our efforts," he said confidently.

At that moment you couldn't have driven a broomstraw up my ass with a sledgehammer. I guess K. Brad sensed my stress.

"There's no reason to be concerned. I'll not be part of harming innocent people. I've never been seduced by the ends-justifies-the-means narcotic. After our meeting in Nacogdoches, I had you under constant surveillance, as much for your safety as mine. It was my men who killed Costillo's people in the parking lot. I apologize for their tardiness in stabilizing the situation that night. I'd hoped to spare you and your friends any injury," he said sincerely.

"I suppose I should thank you," I said, feeling relieved that he didn't appear to have sensed my suspicions.

"Unnecessary," he said quickly.

"Well . . . I guess we've kicked it around long enough," I said, looking him in the eyes. "I've got to take what I know to the authorities or the press or both. I've no choice."

"In the first place, it's not what you know, it's what you suspect—and that distinction is the ball game in this situation. The police will laugh at you and the press will ignore you. Should they not, I have a battery of lawyers poised and ready to request an injunction against any publication. The people in the Department of Corrections will think you insane. All in all, Fowler, I doubt that you will meet with any success."

He seemed too smug, too sure. All of what he said made some sense, but no one with this sort of operation in the works could afford to have someone like me running around trying to queer the deal. The most obvious explanation for this confidence would be my demise. But, if that had been his plan, he could have done it any time. Aside from that, I believed the man when he said we had nothing to fear from him. The only other explanation that made any sense was that I couldn't do anything in time.

That had to be it. He was going to kill them before I could do anything. I had to get the hell out of there.

"What'll become of you and your wife if all this goes off as planned?" I asked.

"Wanda was left comatose from her stroke. She has irreparable brain damage. She'll never regain consciousness. Nothing will ever hurt her again. As for me, I've been living on borrowed time for some time now. Doctors tell me that I ought to be dead already. It seems my heart's shot. We both know why I haven't allowed my heart to stop just yet. I doubt that I'll be around to take any of the heat. But hell, it might get me elected governor."

"It's not too late to call this off," I said, getting up. I needed to get out of there and find Beth.

183

"Fowler, you like to look at the bottom line. Well, consider something before you do anything rash. Bottom line, if you are successful in your efforts, who'll benefit the most? On the other hand, if Paco Costillo is exterminated, who'll benefit the most?" he asked rhetorically.

It's too bad K. Brad Turrow chose business instead of law for his profession. I had a feeling that as a prosecutor he would have made a difference.

"K. Brad . . . you're a piece of work," I said, offering him my hand. He took it and shook it firmly.

"Fowler, when this is all over, win or lose, prove Wolfe wrong. You know, in a couple of months, the leaves will start to change down Nacogdoches way. Someone who really understands why that's important ought to be there to appreciate it," he said as I stepped into the elevator.

As the doors closed, I watched him walk away. I sat down on one of the posh sofas and thought about what I'd been told. I wasn't happy about the choices confronting me. It was a no-win situation. Aside from the moral and ethical considerations, this was the day Jimmy Wayne was supposed to be at the prison. It was clear to me that I couldn't let him die like this.

⏷

23

Getting It Done

I LOOKED OVER THE elevator more closely this time around.
There was a small television camera in the corner. I took a
seat and tried to appear comfortable. My mind was racing
along. What would await me in the lobby? I checked my
watch. It was 3:26. The fastest elevator I'd ever ridden on
seemed to take an hour to reach the lobby. I decided to put
up a hell of a fight, should there be anyone waiting for me.
The lobby approached. I braced myself. Happily, the doors
opened to nothing but cold, blue marble. I scanned the area.
I didn't see anyone who seemed to be interested in me in the
least.

I decided to forgo the underground parking garage. It was
too dark and too empty. I'd leave the car and take a cab. I
walked out the front door and avoided the cab parked at the
curb. The bureau liked to use convenient cabs as surveillance plants. I walked to the corner and hailed one parked a
building over.

"Airport Ramada," I said.

It was 3:40 as we headed east on Travis Street. I wrestled
with whether or not to go directly to Beth or stop along the
way and call her to set up a meeting somewhere else. I figured
that it would take fifteen minutes to get to the motel. The
first five minutes of the drive, I checked for any evidence of
a tail. There was none to be seen. I decided to go directly to
the Ramada. We could use the phone there to contact the
Morrisville facility and we could use her rental car.

Beth was in her room when I got there. I began filling
her in on the meeting as I called Morrisville. The recording
said that there were difficulties with the phones and that

185

every effort was being taken to correct the problem.

"They've cut off communications to and from the prison. It's going down right now." It was 4:03.

"You're sure that he intends to somehow kill all of them?" she asked in disbelief.

"That's precisely what he intends to do," I said as I dialed information for the number of the TDC central offices in Huntsville.

"How . . . how could he possibly pull off killing thousands of men?" she asked.

"I'm not sure, but I think they're going to gas them. The place is equipped with the ability to saturate the entire facility with a debilitating sedative gas at the first sign of any problems with the prison population. My guess is that their security system will indicate some sort of major disturbance and the gas that will be used wouldn't be the kind you wake up from."

When I finally got through to the Hunstville facility, I was met with the same recording I'd encountered at Morrisville.

"We're not going to be able to get through to anyone in the entire system who can do a damn thing," I said as frustration began to take hold.

"How about the cops?" she asked.

"Shit, it'd take two hours to get anyone to stop laughing. Maybe the bureau could get someone's ear," I said as I dialed the Houston number.

"I need to talk to either Agent Corder or Georgis," I explained.

"Neither agent is in the office at the moment. Would you like to leave a message?" the polite voice said.

I left a message that I'd called and told them I'd be at the Morrisville facility by 6:00 P.M. I mentioned that Paco Costillo was going to be killed sometime today.

"Why didn't you try for someone else?" she asked.

"Who'd believe any of this? Besides, we're as close as any of those people anyway. And with the phones down, what could they do that we can't, and faster," I replied, pushing toward the door.

"This is the first time I've ever been pushed out of a motel room," she said as she grabbed her purse.

It was about forty minutes from the motel to Morrisville. Along the way Beth pumped me mercilessly about the meeting with K. Brad. Her mind was factoring all the new information into the weave.

The sign said Morrisville was another twelve miles. The speedometer said ninety-five. The rented Chrysler was about to explode.

As we turned down the long access road that led to the initial checkpoint, I could see a prison transfer bus just in front of us. It looked like an ugly blue whale.

I didn't know if I would get to the main facility in time to do any good, but I could sure as hell see to it that this load was spared. I pulled up alongside and cut them off so sharply that they were forced into the ditch. I figured that a few cuts and bruises were preferable to what awaited them a mile or so down the road.

As we approached the guard booth, he blocked the road. He was armed with a handgun, but it was his clipboard he was sporting.

"Sir, I'll need a pass before I can let you proceed beyond this point," he said as only an armed, fourteen-thousand-dollar-a-year state employee can say it.

"I don't have a pass, but I need to see the warden as soon as possible," I said with all the authority I could muster.

"Well, sir, the phones are down and I can't get anyone to answer my radio calls. Without a verbal authorization from my shift commander, you'll have to produce a written pass to go any farther," he said firmly.

I was about to argue the point more forcefully when I saw the flashing lights coming up behind us. The guard saw them as well and told us to pull over to the right to afford the state vehicles quick access. Six cars were in the caravan. Two were Texas Highway Patrol, three were Texas Rangers, and one was Texas Department of Corrections. The lead car slowed only enough for the driver to flash credentials.

"That means the facility will probably be closed down,"

he told us as the last of the vehicles passed. "Somethin' strange been goin' on up there for the last coupla hours," he mumbled.

"Well, I guess we'll try to see the warden another time," I said, smiling.

The guard grunted and kept his eyes on the vehicles heading for the main gates. I turned the car around and headed back down the road. We passed the bus. Two guards and several inmates were sitting alongside the road. None seemed to be the worse for wear.

"What do you think?" Beth asked.

"I have a feeling that there are a lot of dead men back there."

"My God, I can't believe he did it," she said as we turned onto the main road. At least a dozen police and emergency vehicles passed us going in the opposite direction.

"What are we going to do now?" she asked.

"We're going back to Nacogdoches. The shit's going to hit the fan and we've got some decisions to make."

"Do we have any choices about what to do?" she asked.

"One of the things I didn't have time to tell you is that it was Turrow's people who shot the hitters back in Tommy's parking lot. Their orders were to protect us," I said.

"So we were under his thumb from the Nacogdoches meeting until today," she said thoughtfully.

"That's about the size of it. Any way you cut it, he saved our lives," I said.

"That does cast a different light on the situation, but I don't see how we can help the man regardless of what we do. There's no possible way for him to escape culpability in this."

"Lady, remember where you are. In Texas anything but good government is possible. Money, power, politics, and ambition make an interesting stew. Think about it for a few minutes. The authorities can't afford to admit that they had a lot of the information for several days before the crime took place . . . and did nothing. You can bet your ass that the Department of Corrections won't be rushing to press with a

188

story focusing on their ineptitude. Their best play is a terrible accident angle. They'll produce mismarked gas canisters and some dumb bastard who'll testify that he made the mistake. They'll fire him and he'll retire on his new farm in the hill country. Depending on how Turrow wants to play it, his name might not ever be mentioned," I reasoned.

"That scenario is almost more unbelievable than the act itself," she said, shaking her head at the mere thought. "So what you're saying is that conceivably we have K. Brad's fate in our hands."

"That's about the size of it," I said, giving her plenty of room to respond.

"Thanks. You can be a real prick when you want to."

"That's what my momma used to say. . . . But that's not an answer to the implied question before you."

"I'm a journalist, not a judge or a legislator. We gave K. Brad a choice. We gave him an option. The way I see it, his fate was in his own hands. In making his own choice, he left us no option as to ours. I hope whatever price he pays is just, but my forty-nine percent of the vote is for publication," she said with conviction.

"Forty-nine percent, huh. And you call me a prick," I said with a grin. "I guess that you're going to write a thesis about this."

By the time we pulled into Nacogdoches, the radio news was providing limited information about an accident of catastrophic proportions that had occurred at the Morrisville prison facility. While details were scarce, it appeared that hundreds, perhaps thousands, of inmates had perished.

We went straight to the house and called the hospital. Case was asking about us. I left word that we'd be by a little later to see him.

The television stations were obsessed with the story. Every station had live crews at the site. We watched as various TDC officials were questioned about what had transpired. Finally, a spokesman for the governor, who had personally flown over to inspect the situation, issued a statement that said that several thousand inmates had died when a toxic gas was accidentally released into the prison ventilation system. Culpability for this tragedy had not been determined. A special investigation was in progress.

Beth was telling me that it looked as if my prophecy was becoming a reality when the Morrisville story was interrupted for a newsbrief from Houston. About an hour after the Morrisville accident, an unknown number of gunmen had broken into the Houston mansion of suspected drug lord, Esteban Costillo. Costillo and six of his people had been gunned down.

"I guess K. Brad's closed the loop and found his justice in full measure," I said.

"And at the same time, it takes us out of harm's way," she said quietly.

"We best go over and see Case," I suggested.

The television was on when we entered his room. Case was sitting up in bed watching a Houston newsman detailing the events of the day with Morrisville in the background. He was interviewing a shaken Jimmy Wayne Ellis, who was recounting the events of the day. He'd been in a meeting with prison officials when the catastrophe took place.

I breathed a sigh of relief, but wondered how many men like Jimmy Wayne had died in that prison. But, then again, how many animals would never find their way into society again?

"Close the door," Case suggested and turned off the set.

"What the fuck is goin' on?" he asked, tossing the remote control onto the pillow next to him.

"First things first. How are you doin'?" I asked.

"Hell, I'll be back to work in a couple of weeks or so. Just a few more scars."

Beth and I sat down and invested nearly half an hour in recounting the events of the last couple of days. Case paid total attention. While we talked, he produced a hidden plug from under his pillow.

"Who told you you were all right?" I asked.

"Dr. Freddy, of course," he said. "He's the only doctor I trust," he said, looking for his cup.

"Yeah, well, you might want a second opinion on that. I

190

remember having to help Freddy Schoppe cheat his way through high school anatomy," I pointed out.

"Don't pay any attention to him," Beth said soothingly. "You look better shot up than most men do in perfect condition."

Case looked at me and smiled.

"Forget it, she's just being kind to a dying man who has a quack for a doctor," I said.

He winked at Beth and ignored my comments altogether.

"By the way, what's this hogshit about me shootin' them two Mex hitters in the parkin' lot?" he asked.

"Seemed like the thing to say at the time. I didn't shoot them and I didn't know who did. You'd squeezed off a couple of shots. . . . Telling them you did it saved Beth and me a lot of questions and time," I said matter-of-factly.

"Right," he said, buying none of it. "Course it never occurred to you that such a cock-and-bull story as that might help my election chances. Buck came by this mornin' to tell me that he's withdrawin' from the race. Said they wasn't no fun in winnin' from a man in the hospital. I 'spect he saw the writin' on the wall."

"Another unopposed race," I said with a smile. "Even money you get reelected."

"Kinda strange how things seem to turn out for the best," he said, looking at the television.

"Ain't it the truth," I said.

"You know, Fowler, I'm just a small-town cop. When a man commits a crime, I generally put him in jail. But ever once in a while, it makes better sense to look the other way. Like the time Dooly Martin got Bessie May Sullivan drunk over to the lake and took liberties with her. Now, her brother, Sammy Joe, went over to Dooly's trailer and kicked the everlovin' shit outta ol' Dooly. I coulda arrested Sammy Joe for assault. I coulda arrested Dooly for takin' advantage of a minor. But at the time, it seemed to me that the girl wasn't hurt much and Dooly would recover none the worse for wear. Justice just sorta took care of itself without my gettin' involved," he said as he spit into the cup.

191

"That's an interesting story," I said. "It almost sounds like you think I ought to walk away from this and leave it alone . . . as in, justice has sort of taken care of itself."

"Did that sound that way to you?" he asked, shaking his head. "Sometimes, it's real tough for a country boy to express himself so's he's understood."

"Yeah, I can see how that could be a real problem," I agreed.

The nurse came in and ran us off. When we left, Case was chewing and watching television.

▽

24

Comfort in the Storm

THE NEXT DAY, I found a small package on my doorstep. It was addressed to me with no hint as to the sender. Inside was a cassette tape. The voice on the tape left no doubt who'd sent it.

Fowler, I couldn't leave all this without a couple of last-minute comments. I apologize in advance for not providing you with opportunity for rebuttal. I know that you do not share my enthusiasm for recent events. However, I do want you to know that there were almost two hundred men convicted of capital offenses who were not at Morrisville during the time in question. A battery of legal experts examined the convictions of every capital offender in the state and determined that these men had legitimate grounds for appeal. We saw to it that their transfer to the facility was delayed. I've no regrets. When you write of this, tell it as only you know it to be. I know that some men died in the facility who might've been salvageable, but think of the price society would have to pay to give them a chance. Is it worth letting a hundred animals go in hopes of finding a couple of human beings? Don't allow the events to be distorted beyond recognition. Maximize what good there is in all of this.

When I tried to rewind the tape, I discovered that it had been constructed to erase with rewinding.

One day later, K. Brad Turrow was dead of a heart attack.

The nation mourned his passing without full knowledge of his contributions.

For the next three weeks, Beth commuted between Nacogdoches and Houston. We worked on her thesis, while at the same time collaborating on a book that told the total story behind Morrisville. We titled the book *Rehabilitation: Texas Style*.

A publisher bought the rights to the book. The dollar amounts they threw at us were staggering. I knew how a high school blue-chipper felt after having supper with an A&M recruiter. To promote interest in the book, we wrote a magazine article giving many of the details of the slaughter at Morrisville. K. Brad's involvement was mentioned. These brief revelations sent shock waves throughout the state and the nation. But as K. Brad had predicted, the reason was not wholly condemnatory. It ran the gamut between horror and guilty relief. I heard people attribute Morrisville to everything from God's intervention to the inevitable conspiracy with the federal government. Whether it was ordained, planned, or accidental, a large number of folks felt it was for the best. I still had my doubts.

I had an interesting conversation with Jimmy Wayne. He never took a firm position on the events at Morrisville, but he told me that, philosophical issues aside, society was probably better off for the loss of ninety-five percent of the men in the facility. And, as he pointed out, in two or three years we'd have Morrisville full again. I stopped having my nightmare about the old man and the boy. I see Jimmy Wayne as he is today. I'm finally comfortable with that. I hope Jimmy Wayne's nightmares are gone as well.

Case won reelection without benefit of opposition. A few days after polling day the official forensics report stated that both of the hitmen had died from gunshot wounds from high-powered rifles.

The folks in Nacogdoches ignored the official findings, preferring instead to believe the myth about their sheriff. I guess it just goes to prove that if you want a hero badly enough, facts generally don't get in the way. In a few years, the facts would be forgotten and the myth forever in place. So popular was Case that a move was afoot to have him run for mayor. Local blacks had formed a political action committee and were backing Case for the top office. Ed Andy was approaching terminal pucker.

Each time Beth went back to Houston, our relationship became less tangible to me. We didn't talk about it. Instead, we instinctively tried to enjoy every minute we were together, as if each minute would be our last.

She successfully completed her thesis. Her orals went off flawlessly. The evening of the orals, I came home to find a copy of the thesis sitting in the middle of the poker table.

I went to the bar and got a drink. I sat on the hearth and looked at the thesis sitting there. I had a bad feeling about it. I finally went over and picked it up and went back to my roost. It lay in my lap for several minutes as I looked around the room and thought of the times Beth and I had spent here. Somehow, I knew that when I opened the cover, the mist would appear and Brigadoon would be gone. Finally, I faced the inevitable. There was a note inside the cover.

Fowler, I don't understand this at all. I've always been strong enough to confront my good-byes. This time I just wasn't up to it.

I love you and you know that. You love me and I know that. But lately I've come to understand that being in love doesn't always free a person to do what they would wish to do.

I have responsibilities that I must stand behind. I'm not sure that I can explain it to you. You'll just have to trust me.

The last few weeks have been the best part of my life. No one will ever be able to take them from me. You're the only person who ever put rainbows in my wine. Rainbows, you know, make the storm tolerable. They're not forever things, but after every storm they usually appear.

I closed the book and walked out on the back patio. The wind was picking up and there was an unusual nip in the air. The tallow leaves were already starting to change color. There was a hint of orange on the tips of the larger leaves. The big oaks were starting to sport their yellows and reds. Early color, I'm told, comes from a dry summer and a wet fall. I watched a mallard chase a hen across the lake. The evening light was reflecting off his green neck. I thought about Beth.

"Fowler, we going to play cards or what?" Hob asked as he and Emmet came in the door. I could see Tommy's motorcycle and Case's patrol car coming up the drive. Charlie was sure to be close behind.

"Shit son, get your Hollywood-bound ass in here and fill us in on the movie contract I heard about this afternoon," Emmet exclaimed.

As I closed the French doors I noticed a gathering of clouds to the north. It might be a storm. I hoped so.